"Mary?" Jessica said. "Don't tell me she was here *again*!"

"She wanted to come over," Elizabeth said simply.

"Did you watch how she follows Mom all over the place?" Jessica asked.

Elizabeth didn't answer.

"It's true, isn't it?" Jessica continued. "Mary doesn't care which one of us she comes home with. As long as she can spend time with Mom, she's happy."

"But why should that matter to you?" said Elizabeth.

"It does matter, Lizzie," said Jessica. "I don't happen to want to share my mother. I don't want Mary coming over anymore."

"What do you mean?"

"I mean, I don't think either one of us should invite her over anymore," Jessica said. "I don't like her here, Liz. She gives me the creeps the way she hangs around Mom."

After Jessica left the room, Elizabeth sat quietly for a few minutes. She hoped she'd be able to discourage Mary without too much trouble. After all, Mary was such a nice girl.

SWEET VALLEY TWINS

Three's a Crowd

Written by
Jamie Suzanne

Created by
FRANCINE PASCAL

A BANTAM SKYLARK BOOK®
TORONTO • NEW YORK • LONDON • SYDNEY • AUCKLAND

RL 4, 008–012

THREE'S A CROWD
A Bantam Skylark Book / April 1987

*Sweet Valley High and Sweet Valley Twins are trademarks of
Francine Pascal*

Conceived by Francine Pascal

Produced by Cloverdale Press, Inc.

Cover art by James Mathewuse

*Skylark Books is a registered trademark of Bantam Books, Inc.
Registered in U.S. Patent and Trademark Office and elsewhere.*

ISBN 0-553-15500-8

Published simultaneously in the United States and Canada

*Bantam Books are published by Bantam Books, Inc. Its trade-
mark, consisting of the words "Bantam Books" and the por-
trayal of a rooster, is registered in U.S. Patent and Trademark
Office and in other countries. Marca Registrada. Bantam
Books, Inc., 666 Fifth Avenue, New York, New York 10103.*

PRINTED IN THE UNITED STATES OF AMERICA

O   0 9 8 7 6 5 4 3 2 1

Three's
a
Crowd

One

◇

Janet Howell clapped her hands impatiently. "This meeting of the Unicorns will now come to order," she said. The group of girls sitting around the cafeteria table quickly stopped talking.

Jessica Wakefield, a sixth grader and one of the younger members of the club, sat up attentively. Ever since she'd been asked to join the Unicorns at the beginning of the school year, she'd felt very special. All of the school's most popular girls belonged to the club. Jessica glanced around the table and smiled to herself. Her identical twin, Elizabeth, was probably home by now, curled up with a good book.

With the same long, blond hair and blue-green eyes, Jessica and Elizabeth were so much alike it was nearly impossible to tell them apart. But the two twelve-year-old girls couldn't have been more different. Elizabeth would have nothing to do with the Unicorns. "All they ever do is talk about clothes and boys," she once said. Elizabeth preferred working on *The Sweet Valley Sixers*, the sixth grade newspaper at Sweet Valley Middle School.

Jessica glanced at her friend Ellen Riteman and tapped her foot impatiently. She and Ellen had planned to go shopping at the Valley Mall that afternoon to expand their purple wardrobes. Purple was the Unicorns' favorite color, and Jessica tried to wear at least one purple thing every day. But at the rate this meeting was going, the stores would be closed before they got to the mall.

Janet waited until she was sure she had everyone's attention before she spoke. "We have got to do something about our treasury funds," she began. "There is no way we can sponsor a dance in one month with only thirteen dollars."

Jessica sighed. This was going to take forever. She absolutely hated it when the Unicorns discussed fund-raising. No one could ever agree on a project.

Lila Fowler raised her hand. "I have an easy solution," she said. "Why don't we collect all our old toys and sell them? I have lots that I never even used."

Everyone groaned. Only Lila would keep a roomful of unused toys. The Fowlers were one of the wealthy families in Sweet Valley, and Lila always got whatever she wanted.

Mary Giaccio raised her hand. Although Mary was a seventh grader, she and Jessica had started to spend more time together lately. "How about a celebrity cookbook?" she said. "Each one of us will write to a movie star and ask him or her to send their favorite recipes. We can type them up and sell them."

"What a great idea!" said Janet. The rest of the girls nodded enthusiastically.

Jessica raised her hand. "I'll volunteer to do the typing," she said. "I have an electric typewriter."

"That's terrific, Jessica." Janet beamed. "I didn't know you could type."

Actually, Jessica had no idea of how to type. Elizabeth did, though. Elizabeth had gotten the typewriter for her last birthday. Jessica was sure Elizabeth wouldn't mind helping the Unicorns just this once, and she might even write Jessica's celebrity letter. Jessica already knew whom she wanted to write—Vanessa Brittan, the star of her favorite TV soap opera.

Jessica looked around the table at the smiling faces and felt pleased with herself. She had obviously made another good move.

The Unicorns quickly wrapped things up. "That was a great idea, Mary," said Jessica as she and Ellen hurried out the door.

"Thanks," Mary replied. Mary, who was a foster child, lived with the Altmans down the street from the Wakefields. Although Mary had moved to Sweet Valley only recently, she was well liked by everyone.

Mary watched Jessica and Ellen leave. "Are you going home?" she asked Jessica.

"No, we're going to the mall," Jessica replied. "Want to come?"

Mary shook her head. "Maybe another time," she said.

When Jessica got home, Elizabeth lay reading on the living-room couch. "Hi, Liz," said Jessica. She flopped down on top of her sister's feet.

"Ouch," said Elizabeth, drawing up her legs. "That hurts."

"Sorry, big sister," said Jessica. Elizabeth had been born four minutes before Jessica, so she was the "big sister" and Jessica was the "little sister." It had become a running joke between the twins.

Jessica looked at her sister and grinned. "Any phone calls for me?" she asked.

Elizabeth made a face and put down her book. "Just one," she said. "Janet Howell wanted to know if she could borrow your typewriter to write a letter to Vanessa Brittan."

"But I was going to write to Vanessa!" Jessica protested. "No fair!"

"And whose typewriter was Janet planning to use, anyway?" asked Elizabeth.

Jessica clapped her hand over her mouth. "I'm sorry, Liz," she said. "I would have asked you sooner, but Ellen and I had to go to the mall. You don't mind if Janet uses your typewriter, do you?"

Elizabeth didn't answer.

"And, Liz," Jessica said in a very small voice, "while we're on the subject, would you mind doing a little typing for the Unicorns? I told everyone I would type up the celebrity cookbook we're compiling."

Elizabeth looked at her twin and sighed. Even though she loved Jessica more than anyone, it seemed that her sister was always asking her for something.

"You're such a good typist," Jessica added. "I didn't think you'd mind."

Elizabeth smiled. "How come you always get me into these things?" she said.

"Then you'll do it?" Jessica asked. "I promise never to ask another favor again."

"I'll believe that," Elizabeth said with a grin, "when it happens."

The next afternoon, Jessica was headed across the parking lot when she heard Mary Giaccio call her name.

Jessica turned around and waved.

"Are you going home?" asked Mary.

Jessica nodded. "Want to come?"

"Sure," said Mary. "Maybe we can get Elizabeth to help us write our celebrity letters."

Jessica frowned. "I think Elizabeth is working on *The Sweet Valley Sixers* this afternoon," she said. "The newspaper is planning a special issue for Career Day next month."

"That's OK," Mary replied cheerfully. "We can always listen to records."

Jessica looked down at Mary's wrist. "Oooh," she said. "You're wearing my favorite bracelet again!"

Mary smiled and held out her wrist as they walked toward Jessica's house. She'd had the narrow gold and silver band for as long as she could remember. Every time she wore it, she received lots of compliments.

Mary followed Jessica through the kitchen door. Mrs. Wakefield was sitting at the kitchen table, going through the mail. She worked as an interior designer.

"Hello, Mrs. Wakefield!" Mary beamed.

Mrs. Wakefield put down her mail. "Hello, Mary," she replied. "How have you been?"

"Fine," she said. "Have you heard about the celebrity cookbook we're writing?" Mary started telling Mrs. Wakefield all about her idea.

"Would anyone care for a soda?" Jessica interrupted.

Mrs. Wakefield looked up. "No, thank you." She smiled. She and Mary continued their conversation.

Just then Steven Wakefield barged into the kitchen. "A celebrity cookbook?" he hooted after hearing part of the conversation. "You've got to be joking. Since when do movie stars cook?"

"This happens to be a private conversation, Steven," Jessica said. She squeezed her chair in next to Mary's. Sometimes her brother was the world's biggest pain.

"And why would a movie star want to write to a lowly sixth grader?" Steven continued.

Jessica's eyes narrowed.

"Steven, that's enough," said Mrs. Wakefield. She glanced at the kitchen clock. "Oh, gosh, where did the time go?" she said. "I've got to make some phone calls before the end of the business day." She grabbed her appointment book and left the kitchen.

"Why don't we work on our letters," Mary said. "I'm going to write to Brett Savage. How about you, Jessica?"

"Janet Howell stole Vanessa Brittan from me," Jessica grumbled. "Maybe I'll try Parker Smith. He's cute." Before long, Jessica and Mary were busy composing, and Jessica had forgotten about Steven.

Elizabeth and her best friend, Amy Sutton, burst into the kitchen. "News flash! News flash!" cried Amy as she ran past the table, waving a piece of paper. "Soda and candy machines to be installed in the cafeteria."

Jessica stared in disbelief. "Wait till fatso Lois Waller hears this one," she said.

"Jessica!" Elizabeth protested. "That's not very nice. Anyway, we still don't know if it's really true."

"According to Caroline Pearce, we'll have them by next week," said Amy. Caroline wrote the gossip column for *The Sweet Valley Sixers* and was known to have the inside scoop on everything.

Elizabeth peered over her sister's shoulder. "What are you writing?" she asked.

"Letters to celebrities," Mary replied. "Want to help?"

Elizabeth pointed to Jessica's letter. "You misspelled 'recipe,'" she said with a grin.

"I told you we needed help," Jessica said.

Mrs. Wakefield reentered the room. "I thought I heard a crowd in here," she said.

Mary got up from the table and ran over. "What do you think of my letter?" she asked eagerly.

Mrs. Wakefield quickly scanned the page. "Not bad." She smiled. "Did you know you misspelled 'recipe'?"

The girls burst out laughing.

"What's so funny?" said Mrs. Wakefield.

"Maybe we should give Mary and Jessica a dictionary." Elizabeth chuckled.

Mrs. Wakefield looked at Mary and Amy, and smiled. "Would you two like to stay for dinner?" she asked.

Mary shook her head. "I should probably be going," she said.

"Why don't we meet at your house tomorrow, Mary?" Jessica asked.

Mary hesitated. "We may need Elizabeth's help again," she replied.

"Not if you have a dictionary," joked Amy.

"What about a typewriter?" Mary added. "I know Mrs. Altman doesn't own one." *Mrs. Altman was Mary's foster mother.*

Jessica shrugged. "Then I guess we'll meet here."

That evening, Jessica knocked on Elizabeth's door. "What's up?" asked Elizabeth.

Jessica threw herself down on the end of Elizabeth's bed. "Tell me if this sounds OK," she said. She held up a piece of paper and began to read. "'Dear Parker, *Love and Lace* is my favorite TV show, and naturally you are my favorite actor. I'm writing to you because my club, the Unicorns, is sponsoring a dance next month, and we're broke. To raise money, we're putting together a celebrity cookbôok. I hear you're a pretty good cook. Would you mind sending us a few of your favorite recipes? Also, how about an autographed picture for my wall? Is it true you're not married? Sincerely, your fan, Jessica Wakefield.'"

Jessica stared at Elizabeth hopefully. "What do you think?" she asked.

"It sounds fine except for one thing," said Elizabeth. "I think Parker Smith just married Vanessa Brittan."

Jessica gasped and fell back on the bed. "You're kidding!" she said. She looked at her sister suspiciously. "Liz, are you sure?" she said. "You never pay attention to movie stars."

"It's called 'reading.'" Elizabeth laughed. "You should try it sometime."

Jessica carefully crossed out the sentence about marriage and over it she wrote, "What's it like to be married to another famous celebrity?"

Jessica handed the letter to Elizabeth. "Now it's perfect," she said. "Can you type it?"

"Not right now," Elizabeth said. "I need to write this story for the newspaper about Career Day by tomorrow."

Jessica's face dropped. "It'll only take a minute," she said.

Elizabeth sighed. Couldn't Jessica see she was busy? "I'll make a deal," she said. "I'm supposed to call Mr. Bowman right now to get some information for my story." Mr. Bowman, an English teacher at Sweet Valley Middle School, was the faculty adviser for the sixth-grade newspaper.

Jessica would do anything to get that letter finished. "I'll do it," she said with a smile. "Just give me the phone number."

Elizabeth wrote down the number. Jessica dashed to the phone in the upstairs hallway and dialed.

"Mr. Bowman?" said Jessica. "This is Elizabeth Wakefield."

"Right," he replied. "Here are the dates you need to know. Career Day is on the seventeenth. Our special guests will be David Tower of Consolidated Trucking, June Abraham of Food Industries . . ."

Jessica looked around for a pencil. No luck. She'd just have to remember what Mr. Bowman was saying.

". . . Jane Adams of Pet World, John Jenkins of Miller Design, Henry Weir of Jewelry Mart . . ."

Jessica concentrated as hard as she could, but she was starting to become confused. Was Mr. Weir from Jewelry Mart or Miller Design?

"Do you have that?" Mr. Bowman said.

"I think so," Jessica replied.

"Good," said Mr. Bowman. "Gretchen Tyler from Sweet Valley Fashions . . ."

Jessica stopped listening. *Gretchen Tyler! She owns the Unicorns' favorite clothing store in the mall. Wait till the Unicorns heard about this!*

"One more thing," said Mr. Bowman. "Students must sign up for the career person they wish to visit by the fourteenth."

"Fine," said Jessica. "I'll tell Eliz . . . I mean, I'll be sure to write it all down." She hung up the phone and quickly redialed. "Hello, Lila?" she said. "Guess who's going to be at Career Day?"

In the other room, Elizabeth looked at the neatly typed letter to Parker Smith and smiled. She loved her typewriter more than anything. It was fun to use, and it made her feel like a real writer. Elizabeth glanced out in the hallway. What was taking Jessica so long? She should have been off the phone by now.

Just then, Jessica burst into the room. "Gretchen Tyler is coming to Career Day!" she said. "I can't wait to sign up for her. Wouldn't it be wonderful to have a career in fashion?" She threw herself on Elizabeth's bed and stared dreamily at the ceiling.

"What else did Mr. Bowman say?" Elizabeth asked impatiently. She took a pen and pad of paper from her desk and waited.

Jessica bit her lip. "Let's see," she began. "Career Day will be the fourteenth." She hesitated. "Was it the fourteenth or the seventeenth? Make that the seventeenth," she said.

Elizabeth stopped. "Are you sure?" she asked.

Jessica nodded. "Positive." She took a deep breath. "The other guests will be David Abraham of Consolidated Trucking, Henry Miller of Jenkins Design, Mr. Weir of Jewelry Mart . . ."

"What is Mr. Weir's first name?" said Elizabeth, scribbling furiously.

"John," said Jessica. She couldn't believe she was remembering everything so well. She confidently finished giving the list of names to Elizabeth.

"When should people sign up?" said Elizabeth.

"By the twelfth," said Jessica. "Definitely by the twelfth."

Elizabeth smiled gratefully. "Thanks, Jess," she said. "I really appreciate this." She handed Jessica the neatly typed letter and matching envelope.

Jessica kissed the back of the envelope. "No problem." She grinned. "A favor for a favor, right?" She hurried off to find a stamp.

Two

◇

"Jessica, wait up," shouted Mary.

Jessica shifted her books from one arm to the other. They felt as though they weighed about a ton.

"Can I still come over today?" Mary asked breathlessly.

"Sure," said Jessica.

"I have to stop by my house first," said Mary. "I forgot my letter."

"Fine by me," said Jessica. "I finished mine last night." She gave Mary a significant look. "Did you know Parker Smith is married to Vanessa Brittan?"

"Of course," Mary replied. "Doesn't everybody?"

The girls strolled up the spacious walk to the Altmans' front door. "Wait here," said Mary. "I'll be out in a minute."

Jessica sat down on the doorstep. Several minutes passed.

The door opened. "Mary?" said Mrs. Altman.

Jessica stood up. "Hi, Mrs. Altman," she said. "It's Jessica Wakefield. Mary will be down in a minute. We're going over to my house to finish our celebrity letters."

Mrs. Altman looked puzzled. "Celebrity letters?" she said.

"Didn't Mary tell you?" said Jessica. "The Unicorns are compiling a celebrity cookbook."

Mary hurried out the door. "Hi, Nancy," she said.

Jessica thought it sounded funny to hear someone call Mrs. Altman "Nancy."

Mrs. Altman smiled. "Jessica just told me about your celebrity cookbook," she said. "You'll have to show me your letter when you're finished."

"OK," said Mary. She turned to Jessica. "We'd better get going," she said. "I still have lots to write."

Mrs. Wakefield was in the kitchen when Mary and Jessica walked in. "I see my cookbook experts have arrived," she said.

Mary put her book bag down on the kitchen table and ran over to the sink. "Hi, Mrs. Wakefield. What are you making?" she asked.

"Broccoli soufflé," said Mrs. Wakefield.

"Mmm," said Mary. "That sounds delicious."

Jessica tried not to gag. She hated broccoli soufflé.

"You should tell Nancy to make this dish,"

said Mrs. Wakefield as she chopped the broccoli. "I hear she's a wonderful cook."

"She is?" said Jessica. "How come I've never been invited over to dinner?"

"I don't know." Mary shrugged. She leaned her elbows on the counter. "Can I help you do anything, Mrs. Wakefield?" she asked.

Mrs. Wakefield smiled. "You can chop up that onion if you'd like," she said.

"What about your letter, Mary?" interrupted Jessica.

"I'll work on it later." Mary shrugged again.

"Would you like to grate the cheese, Jessica?" said Mrs. Wakefield.

Jessica made a face. She hated to cook, but she knew it would be impolite to desert her guest. "I guess so," she said. As Jessica grated the cheese, she watched Mary and her mother talk. It seemed that Mary never took her eyes off Mrs. Wakefield.

"May I beat the egg whites?" Mary said.

Jessica sighed. She'd much rather be watching music videos or listening to albums right now.

Finally, the soufflé was ready for the oven.

"Let's go watch some TV," said Jessica.

Mary lingered around the sink.

"Go on, girls," said Mrs. Wakefield. "I'll clean up."

Mary picked up a dirty pan. "That's OK, Mrs. Wakefield," she said. "This only takes a minute."

Jessica couldn't believe it. Was Mary here to see her or to wash dishes? "I'll be watching TV," Jessica said loudly. She stalked into the den and threw herself down on the couch. She'd had enough of cooking.

In Mr. Bowman's room at Sweet Valley Middle School, Elizabeth proudly held up the master sheets for the next edition. "Perfect!" she said. "Start the presses!"

Amy Sutton, Julie Porter, and Caroline Pearce applauded.

"Good work, girls," said Mr. Bowman. "Have you done a final proofreading?"

Elizabeth nodded. As editor, she'd put a lot of time into this issue. It had been her idea to have the newspaper cover Career Day. Elizabeth handed the ditto masters to Mr. Bowman.

"I'll try to get these run off right now so we can staple and distribute them tomorrow," said Mr. Bowman.

"Elizabeth," he called as the girls were leaving. "Do you have a minute?"

Amy, Caroline, and Julie gave Elizabeth a "look" as they scurried out the door. Sometimes they could be so immature, Elizabeth thought.

Mr. Bowman shuffled a few papers around on his desk. "I wanted to tell you what a terrific job you've been doing as editor." He smiled. "I think we have a really top-notch newspaper."

"Thanks." Elizabeth grinned.

Mr. Bowman handed her a piece of paper. "Are you familiar with the Los Angeles Newspaper Guild?" he asked.

Elizabeth shook her head.

"Every year the guild sponsors a competition

for school newspapers," he said. "The prize for the best middle school newspaper is one hundred dollars. I think we have a good shot at winning."

Elizabeth was speechless. *The Sweet Valley Sixers* a statewide winner! What an honor that would be! "What do we need to do to enter?" she said eagerly.

"The first step is to submit a recent issue," Mr. Bowman replied. He held up the master. "I think this issue will make a good entry, don't you?"

Elizabeth nodded happily. "Wait until I tell the other girls!"

When Elizabeth got home, she found Jessica watching TV in the den. "Where's everyone else?" she said.

"How should I know?" Jessica said crossly.

Elizabeth ran into the kitchen. "Hi, Mary. Hi, Mom," she said. What was Mary doing there? "Mom, guess what! We're entering *The Sweet Valley Sixers* in a school newspaper competition. Mr. Bowman thinks we're good enough to win!"

"Elizabeth! That's wonderful!" said her mother. "I'm really proud of you."

Elizabeth beamed. "Also, I'm staying late tomorrow at school. Amy and Julie are throwing a surprise birthday party for Mr. Bowman after we finish distributing the paper. Caroline Pearce found out he's going to be twenty-seven years old."

Mrs. Wakefield laughed. "How in the world did she discover that?"

"He went to high school with Mrs. Pearce's younger sister," Elizabeth replied. "You should see his old yearbook picture. He had *really* long hair and glasses."

Elizabeth suddenly stopped talking and stared at Mary. "Are you doing *dishes?*" she said.

"I'm almost finished," Mary replied. "I'm just helping your mom."

Mrs. Wakefield dried her hands with a dish towel. "We should have Mary over more often." She grinned. "Don't you agree?"

That evening, Elizabeth was tackling a difficult math problem when Jessica barged through the door. "Liz, Janet Howell just called," she said. "She's coming over tomorrow to use the typewriter."

"But it's not here," said Elizabeth. "I took it to school today to type up the newspaper. That old manual one we used to use was just the worst!"

"But I *promised* Janet," Jessica said. "Can't you bring it home tomorrow?" said Jessica.

Elizabeth shook her head. "I'm staying late after school," she replied. "It's Mr. Bowman's birthday."

"No problem," Jessica persisted. "I'll pick it up myself. Just tell me where you left it."

Elizabeth put down her pencil. Sometimes Jessica could be so demanding. "Meet me in Mr. Bowman's room at three o' clock," she said.

Jessica hugged her sister. "Thanks a million times, Liz," she said. "I promise I'll take really good care of it."

The next afternoon, Jessica was hurrying to Mr. Bowman's room when she ran into Mary.

Mary seemed really happy to see Jessica. "Where are you going?" she asked. "I haven't seen you today."

"I have to pick up my typewriter," Jessica replied. "Elizabeth borrowed it yesterday to type the newspaper."

Mary smiled shyly. "Do you need help carrying it home?" she asked.

Jessica hesitated. "That's OK," she said. "I can manage. Janet is coming over this afternoon to type up her letter."

Mary lingered by Jessica's side. "I need to type *my* letter too," she said.

"Janet is a pretty slow typist," said Jessica. "It may take her a long time."

"That's OK," Mary replied. "I can always do something else while I'm waiting."

Mary followed Jessica into Mr. Bowman's room. Elizabeth was standing on a desk, hanging crepe paper streamers. "Hi, Jess. Hi, Mary," she said. "Good thing both of you showed up. This typewriter weighs a ton."

Before Jessica could say anything, Mary rushed over and picked the typewriter up. "Come on, Jessica," she said. "We don't want to miss Janet."

Twenty minutes later, Mary and Jessica struggled through the Wakefields' kitchen door.

"Anybody home?" called Jessica. There was no response.

As Jessica set the typewriter on the kitchen table, she suddenly realized that she'd forgotten to ask Elizabeth how to use it. She wasn't even sure how to get the case open. Jessica fiddled with the latch for several minutes. "Here we go," she said finally. She removed the typewriter from its case and to her despair found no manual.

The front doorbell rang. "That must be Janet," said Mary. "I'll get it."

Jessica could hear lots of voices in the front hallway. Mary reappeared with Janet, Betsy Gordon, and Tamara Chase. Betsy and Tamara were seventh grade members of the Unicorns.

"Hi, Jessica," Janet said. "You don't mind if Betsy and Tamara use your typewriter, do you?"

"No problem," said Jessica. She glanced nervously at the kitchen table. What if someone asked her to type something? What was she going to say?

Janet had already sat down at the typewriter. "How do you use this thing?" she said.

Jessica panicked. "Simple," she said. "You just plug it in and type."

Janet inserted a piece of paper. "Will you help me?" she said. "I'm not used to an electric typewriter."

Jessica held out her hand apologetically. "I can't," she replied. "I jammed my finger in gym class today."

"How did you do that?" said Tamara.

Jessica thought fast. "Lois Waller ran into me," she replied. "What a tub." Everyone except Janet burst out laughing.

"I hope you're still going to type the recipes," Janet said. "The Unicorns are counting on you."

"Oh, sure," Jessica replied quickly. The last

thing she wanted to do was get on Janet's bad side. Janet was president of the Unicorns, and her opinion really mattered.

Mrs. Wakefield came through the back door carrying a stack of wallpaper samples. "Celebrity cookbook time?" she asked, smiling.

"Hi, Mrs. Wakefield," chorused the girls.

Mary rushed over. "Let me help you with those," she said.

"Thank you, Mary," said Mrs. Wakefield. "You're getting to be indispensible around here."

Jessica's eyes narrowed. Why was Mary paying so much attention to her mother? In all the time that Mary and Jessica had been friends, Mary had never once invited Jessica over to her house. She never wanted to go shopping or to the movies, either. All Mary ever wanted to do was come over to Jessica's house, especially if she knew Jessica's mother would be there.

"Jessica, your stupid typewriter isn't working right," said Janet. "Look. The keys are all jammed up."

Jessica leaned over the keyboard and gasped. What had Janet done? The inside of Elizabeth's typewriter was a hopeless mess.

"It looks broken to me," said Tamara.

Jessica couldn't believe it. Elizabeth was going to kill her. "It wasn't broken before," she said. "It was working perfectly yesterday."

"Don't blame me," said Janet. "I asked you how to use it, and you wouldn't help me."

"But I hurt my hand," said Jessica.

Just then, Elizabeth burst into the kitchen.

She looked really angry. "Jessica," she said in a stifled voice, "I need to talk to you in the other room."

Jessica stared at her sister. It wasn't like Elizabeth to be this upset. Something must really be wrong. "I'll be right back," she told her friends. She followed her twin into Mr. Wakefield's study and shut the door.

"I thought I could trust you to at least get your facts straight, Jess," Elizabeth said angrily.

"What are you talking about?" said Jessica.

"The article I wrote about Career Day," Elizabeth replied. "You mixed up the dates and names that Mr. Bowman gave you. Now we have to completely retype the paper. I feel like a real idiot. I didn't even get to stay for Mr. Bowman's birthday party."

Jessica felt awful. "I'm sorry, Lizzie," she said. "I really am. I could have sworn I got the names right."

Elizabeth sighed loudly. "It's OK. I know you didn't do it on purpose." She smiled at her sister. "Good thing you brought my typewriter home," she said. "I'm going to have to retype everything tonight. The deadline for the competition entry is tomorrow."

"It is?" Jessica gulped.

Elizabeth nodded. "Is something the matter?" she asked.

Jessica glanced nervously toward the kitchen. "I hope not," she said.

Three

◈

Jessica rushed back into the kitchen. All the girls were still huddled over Elizabeth's typewriter. "Is it working yet?" she said anxiously.

"Would everybody please stand back?" snapped Janet. "I can't see."

Jessica peered over Tamara's shoulder. The typewriter still looked hopelessly jammed.

"What's going on?" said Mary as she approached the kitchen table.

Jessica pointed to the typewriter.

"That's easy enough to fix," Mary said cheerfully. She stuck her fingers down into the machine and fiddled with a few of the parts. A minute later, the typewriter was clear. Mary put another sheet of paper in and expertly typed a few lines. "Done," she said.

The girls were speechless.

"Where did you learn to repair typewriters?" said Betsy.

"And when did you learn to type?" added Jessica.

Mary shrugged. "I just picked it up," she said. "It wasn't that hard to fix. A few of the keys were stuck together, that's all."

Jessica was puzzled. There were so many things about Mary that were a mystery. Why hadn't she told anyone she could type? That was the strange thing about Mary. As popular as she was, no one knew very much about her.

Mary invited herself over again the following day just as Jessica had expected. Jessica didn't understand why Mary always wanted to come over, and she didn't like it one bit. This time, though, she was prepared.

"Sorry, Mary," she said. "I'm going over to Ellen's."

Mary looked upset.

Jessica paused. Maybe Mary was just feeling left out. "Would you like to come with us?" she asked. "I'm sure Ellen won't mind."

"I don't think so," Mary responded. "I should probably work on my social studies report."

Jessica smiled to herself. So far, her suspicions were correct. Mary wanted to be around Jessica only if she could spend time with Mrs. Wakefield.

Later, as Jessica and Ellen sat around Ellen's living room, drinking diet soda and eating potato chips, Jessica mentioned Mary's name. "Does Mary ever come over to your house?" she asked casually.

"Sometimes," Ellen said. "Why?"

"Does she like to spend a lot of time in the kitchen, talking to your mom?" Jessica continued.

Ellen looked at her as if she were crazy. "What are you talking about?" she said.

"Never mind," said Jessica. "I was just curious."

When Elizabeth heard the last bell, she quickly gathered her things and got ready to go home. All day she'd had trouble keeping her eyes open. She'd stayed up until almost midnight the night before, doing homework and retyping the newspaper. Mr. Bowman had been upset with Elizabeth when he'd read her article about Career Day. He kept saying that it wasn't like Elizabeth to be so careless. Elizabeth was glad for the chance to make it up, especially if it meant meeting the competition deadline. Good thing Amy, Julie, and Caroline had volunteered to do the stapling and collating this afternoon without her!

As she shut her locker, Elizabeth heard someone call her name. "Hi, Mary," she said.

"You walking home?" asked Mary.

Elizabeth nodded. "I'm exhausted," she said. "I stayed up really late last night."

Mary fell into step with Elizabeth. "Were you retyping the paper?" Mary asked.

"How did you know?" said Elizabeth.

"I overheard your conversation with Jessica yesterday," Mary confessed. "I was on my way back to the kitchen." She smiled at Elizabeth. "You know, I'm a pretty good typist," she said. "If you ever need help again with something, just let me know."

"Wow, thanks, Mary," said Elizabeth. "That's really nice of you." Elizabeth and Mary talked until they reached the Wakefields' doorstep.

Mary craned her neck. "Looks like your mom is home," she said.

"You want to come in for a minute?" said Elizabeth.

"Sure," said Mary. She followed Elizabeth through the back door.

When Jessica got home from Ellen's house about an hour later, the first person she saw when she walked into her kitchen was Mary Giaccio.

Jessica felt her stomach tighten. What was she *doing* here?

"Hi, Jessica," said Mary. "I walked home with Elizabeth today, so she invited me in for a while."

"I don't see Elizabeth." Jessica controlled her voice.

"She just went upstairs to take a nap before dinner," said Mrs. Wakefield. "Mary offered to help with dinner again."

That figures, thought Jessica.

"Do you want to clean the mushrooms, dear?" said Mrs. Wakefield.

Jessica made a face. She was beginning to wonder if she was going to spend the rest of her life in the kitchen with her mother and Mary.

Mary dried her hands with the dish towel. "I've got to be going," she said. "Nancy is probably wondering what happened to me." She turned to Jessica and smiled. "I finally finished my letter to Brett Savage," she said. "Maybe tomorrow I can come over and type it."

Mary seemed so nice, so sincere. Even though Jessica was angry, she knew it was impossible to say no. "All right. I'll see you after school," she muttered.

Mary practically danced out the kitchen door. "Good night, Mrs. Wakefield. Good night, Jessica," she said. "Tell Elizabeth I said goodbye."

Mrs. Wakefield watched Mary leave and smiled. "Mary's such a nice girl," she said. "We should have her over more often."

When Jessica got home the following afternoon, Mary was already sitting at the kitchen table, talking to Mrs. Wakefield.

"Hi, Jessica," Mary said. "I looked for you all over school after the bell rang today."

"You must not have looked that hard," Jessica replied crossly. "I was there."

Mrs. Wakefield cleared her throat. "Did you have a nice day?" she asked.

"It was OK," Jessica replied. She yanked open the refrigerator door and grabbed at a container of milk. Out of the corner of her eye she watched as Mary read her celebrity letter to Mrs. Wakefield.

Mary was reading a sentence about how she'd heard that Brett was into health foods when Steven appeared out of nowhere and planted himself in front of the open refrigerator door. "I thought Brett Savage only ate Wheat Toasties," he said as he attacked the last wedge of apple pie.

"Hungry, Steven?" Jessica asked sarcastically.

"I'm a growing boy," Steven shot back.

"The least you could do is shut the refrigerator door," Jessica said.

"Why should I?" Steven replied. "This way I don't have to get a plate dirty."

Mrs. Wakefield looked over. "Steven," she said, "close the door."

Steven slammed the door shut. "Big mouth," he told Jessica.

Jessica folded her arms against her chest and angrily leaned against the sink. Why wasn't anyone paying attention to her? She peeked back over at her mother and Mary. Mrs. Wakefield was telling Mary how she met Mr. Wakefield.

Jessica almost choked. "Haven't we heard that story before?" she said loudly.

Mrs. Wakefield looked surprised. "Mary hasn't heard it yet," she said.

The phone rang. "I'll get it," Steven shouted. He practically knocked Jessica over as he lunged for the receiver. "It's some client for you, Ma," he said.

"*Ma?*" said Mrs. Wakefield. She picked up her appointment book. "I'll take it in my room."

After Mrs. Wakefield left, Mary got up from the table and walked over to Jessica. "Your mom is really nice," she said.

"I've noticed," said Jessica.

For an instant, Mary looked hurt. "I'll go get the typewriter," she said. "Where is it?"

"In Elizabeth's room," Jessica said.

Mary returned a couple of minutes later.

"Does Elizabeth like horses?" she asked. "She has lots of pictures of them."

"Elizabeth *loves* horses," Jessica replied. "My parents said that if she wants to, she can start taking riding lessons again in a few weeks."

"Lila might be getting a horse," Mary said. "Her father said he'd buy her one."

"Wait till Elizabeth hears that," said Jessica.

When Mrs. Wakefield returned to the kitchen much later, Mary got up from the table and ran over. "I want to hear the rest of the story about you and Mr. Wakefield," she said.

Jessica pursed her lips. Didn't Mary know how to take a hint? "Mary, how did *your* parents meet?" she asked.

There was an uncomfortable silence. "I—I'm not sure," Mary replied.

"Did you finish typing your letter, Mary?" asked Mrs. Wakefield, quickly changing the subject.

Mary nodded. "I guess I should be going," she said. She gathered her things together.

"When are you going to take us up on our dinner invitation?" Mrs. Wakefield asked Mary gently.

"I can't tonight," Mary replied.

"Another time, then," said Mrs. Wakefield.

Mary perked up. "How about tomorrow?"

Jessica clenched her fist. Mary had done it again!

"Fine," said Mrs. Wakefield. "We'll be expecting you."

That night, as Jessica lay in bed, she tried to think of some way to discourage Mary from coming over. It just wasn't fair that Mary spent so much time at their house. What was the matter with the Altmans? If there were just some way to prevent Mary's coming over without hurting her feelings . . .

Jessica suddenly sat up in bed. She had thought of the perfect excuse.

When the final bell rang the next day, Jessica hurried through the corridor to find Mary. Not even Bruce Patman, the cutest boy in the seventh grade, could slow her down.

"Where's the fire?" Bruce shouted as Jessica raced past him.

At the other end of the hall, Jessica spotted Mary. "Mary, wait up," Jessica called.

Mary turned around. Jessica got ready for her performance. She let her face sag and her eyelids droop and then she clutched her stomach tightly.

"What's the matter?" asked Mary. "You don't look very good."

"I think I have one of those stomach viruses," Jessica moaned.

Mary looked worried. "Is it contagious?" she asked.

"I don't know," Jessica replied. "It just came over me about five minutes ago. I feel like throwing up."

"Well, maybe I shouldn't come over," Mary said.

Jessica shook her head sadly. "Maybe you shouldn't," she agreed. She suddenly clapped her hand over her mouth. "Oops," she said. "Gotta go." She hurried out the door and across the parking lot. When she reached the road, she glanced behind her. Mary was nowhere to be seen.

"Anybody home?" called Jessica as she walked in the Wakefields' back door. There was no answer. Jessica looked to see if her mother had left a note on the kitchen table. Since she didn't find one, she figured her mother was probably just running late. Maybe this would be a good time for her to look for that purple knee sock that was lost somewhere in her room. That way her mother wouldn't come in and say something about her messy room.

Jessica pushed open her bedroom door and sighed. It was a wonder she ever found anything in this room. There were clothes, albums, hair bands, and cookie crumbs everywhere. She lifted up a pile of things that had been sitting on a chair and began sifting through them.

Just then Elizabeth burst through the door. "Jess, are you OK?" she asked. "Mary told me that you're sick."

"I'm feeling much . . ." Jessica did a double take as she ran into the hallway at the top of the stairs. Standing behind Elizabeth was Mary! ". . . worse." Jessica sighed. She couldn't believe it.

"I told Mary that she could come over anyway," Elizabeth said. "We're going to bake cookies together. Too bad you don't feel well enough to have any."

"Right," Jessica groaned.

"Can we get you anything?" Mary said cheerfully. "Sometimes soda helps settle your stomach."

All Jessica could think about was crawling into bed and pulling her pillow over her head. "I think I just want to be left alone," she said. So much for her brilliant plan!

Four

◇

A few days later Elizabeth and Amy were sitting on the cafeteria stage after school, discussing their plans for Career Day.

Amy put down her pencil and lay on her back. "Have you ever looked at the stage from this view?" she said. "I never noticed how many lights were up there."

Elizabeth glanced absentmindedly at the ceiling. "Would you like to report on Mr. Weir, Ms. Abraham, and Mr. Jenkins?" she asked.

"Sounds fine," Amy replied. She lay very still. "Did you notice Mr. Bowman's new tie?" she said. "He told us that his mother bought it for him, but I don't believe it. I think he has a girlfriend that he isn't telling us about."

"Maybe he bought the tie himself," said Elizabeth.

"No way," said Amy. "His taste isn't that good."

"Hi, Amy and Elizabeth," interrupted Lois. She lumbered over to the stage. "Are you working on the paper?"

Amy nodded. "We're almost done," she said.

Lois peered around the empty cafeteria. "Anything going on in here?" she asked.

Elizabeth shook her head. "Not that I know of. Why?"

Lois shifted her weight from one foot to the other. "I heard something about candy machines being installed today," she said.

Amy sat up. "That's right!" she said. "Where are they?"

Ms. Wyler, the math teacher, walked past. "Ms. Wyler," said Amy, "what time are the soda and candy machines being installed?"

Ms. Wyler laughed. "That's a good one," she said as she hurried by.

Amy looked at Elizabeth. "Do you think Caroline could have made a mistake?"

Elizabeth grinned. "I told you so," she said.

Amy lay back down on the stage. "That's too bad." She sighed. "I was really working up an appetite for a candy bar."

"Me too," Lois chimed in.

"We can go to my house," Elizabeth said. "We have lots of good stuff in our refrigerator—that is if Steven hasn't eaten it all." Amy and Lois nodded enthusiastically.

As Elizabeth collected her things, she noticed Mary pass by. "Hi, Mary," she called. "How's it going?"

Mary seemed glad to see Elizabeth. "What are you doing?" she asked.

"We're going over to my house," Elizabeth said. "Want to come?"

Mary nodded happily.

Jessica got back from Lila's house around dinnertime. For the past several days, she'd managed to avoid having Mary come over by spending all her time at Lila's or Ellen's.

As the Wakefields sat down to dinner, Mr. Wakefield looked around the table at his family. "What did everyone do today?" he asked.

Steven was busy helping himself to potatoes. "Basketball practice," he grunted.

"I was at Lila Fowler's house," Jessica said. "She just got a whole bunch of new videotapes."

"Amy, Lois, and Mary were here this afternoon," Elizabeth said. "We mostly sat around in the kitchen."

Jessica almost choked on her steak. "*Mary* was here again?" she said. "Who invited her over?"

"I did," said Elizabeth. "What's the big deal?"

Jessica gave Elizabeth an exasperated look. Mary had some nerve, she thought. She obviously didn't care *who* invited her over, just as long as she got to spend time at the Wakefields'.

"What's the matter, Jessica?" teased Steven. "Your face is turning red."

"Mind your own business," she snapped.

"Is little Jessie jealous?" said Steven.

"Of course not," said Jessica.

"Steven, that's enough," said Mrs. Wakefield. "I'm sure Jessica doesn't mind that Mary occasionally comes over with Elizabeth. Do you, darling?"

Jessica couldn't believe this conversation. Why was everybody missing the point. Wasn't it obvious that the only person Mary really wanted to see was Mrs. Wakefield? "Will everyone stop picking on me?" she said. "I don't want to discuss this right now."

Elizabeth looked at her sister and felt a twinge of guilt. Maybe Jessica was angry that she'd invited Mary over. She decided that she'd speak to Jessica privately after dinner.

A short time later, Elizabeth dropped by Jessica's room. "Jess," she called, "where are you?"

Jessica poked her head out of the closet. "Have you seen my pink sweater?" she asked.

"No," Elizabeth said, "but keep looking. It's probably here somewhere." Elizabeth was relieved that Jessica didn't seem angry with her.

Jessica cleared a path out of the closet. "What's up?" she asked.

"You don't care that I invited Mary over today, do you?" Elizabeth said. "I know she was your friend first."

Jessica paused. "That's not what's bothering me," she replied. "It's Mary."

"What about her?" said Elizabeth.

"Have you ever noticed how much time she spends talking to Mom?" Jessica asked.

Elizabeth seemed surprised. "Not really," she said.

"It's true," said Jessica. "Whenever Mom is in the room, Mary ignores everyone else. It's as if no one else matters."

"Are you sure?" said Elizabeth.

Jessica's arms dropped at her side. "Why don't you believe me?" she said. "All Mary cares about is talking to Mom. She doesn't even want to be here when Mom's not here."

Elizabeth looked at her sister and sighed. Once Jessica had made up her mind, it was hard to convince her otherwise. "Maybe Mary wishes she had a mother like ours," she said.

"There's nothing the matter with Mrs. Altman," Jessica replied stubbornly. "Why doesn't she spend time with *her*?"

Elizabeth didn't say anything.

"The next time Mary invites herself over," Jessica continued, "you watch and see who she follows around the whole time."

"OK, OK," said Elizabeth. "If it means that much to you, I will."

Jessica let out a sigh. "Thanks, Liz," she said. "You'll see I'm not crazy."

The next afternoon, Elizabeth and Amy were sitting around Mrs. Bowman's room after school. "Any news from the Newspaper Guild, Mr. Bowman?" said Elizabeth.

Mr. Bowman looked up from the papers he was grading. "Nothing yet," he said.

Amy peered over Mr. Bowman's shoulder.

"You gave Lila Fowler a D on her essay?" She grinned. "Why are you asking for trouble?"

Mr. Bowman covered Lila's grade with his hand. "These marks are supposed to be confidential, Amy," he said.

Amy wasn't the least bit rattled. "Is my essay in there?" she asked.

"You don't want to see it." Mr. Bowman laughed.

Amy's face fell. "Did I get a bad grade?" she asked. "I worked really hard on it."

"Amy," Mr. Bowman said, "you'll find out your grade with the rest of the class."

Elizabeth looked up and saw Mary enter the room. "There you are," Mary said in a relieved voice. "I thought maybe I'd missed you."

"We're helping Mr. Bowman grade papers," joked Amy.

Mary peered at the stack of essays. "Is my book report in there?" she asked.

"You'll find out your grade with the rest of your class," said Amy and Elizabeth in unison. They both burst out laughing.

"Are you going home soon, Elizabeth?" said Mary.

Elizabeth remembered her conversation with Jessica. *It's true,* she thought. *Mary is inviting herself over.* Still, it didn't bother Elizabeth. Mary was always nice to have around. "I guess Mr. Bowman could use some peace and quiet," she said.

"You could say that again," said Mr. Bowman.

*   *   *

No one was home yet when Jessica walked in after school. She was on her way over to the kitchen table to see if her mother had left a note when she noticed the large white envelope addressed to Ms. Jessica Wakefield that was sitting on top of the mail. She grabbed the envelope and opened it.

Inside was a large black-and-white glossy of Parker Smith that said "To Jessica, Love, Parker." There was also a typewritten letter. Jessica picked it up and read it aloud.

"'Dear Jessica, Thank you for your nice letter. Your celebrity cookbook sounds like a fabulous idea. I'm enclosing Van's and my favorite recipe for sweet 'n' sour barbecued ribs. Good luck with your cookbook. Love, Parker. P.S. Being married to Vanessa is heavenly.'"

Jessica sat down and sighed. Parker Smith could be so romantic. Wait until the Unicorns heard about this! A personal letter!

Jessica quickly called Lila. "Lila?" she said. "You won't believe what I just got in the mail. Can I come over right now and show you?" Within minutes, Jessica had left the house, still clutching the white envelope.

Several minutes later, Elizabeth, Mary, and Amy walked into the Wakefields' and threw their things on the kitchen table. "I guess no one's home," Elizabeth said. "Come on. I want to show you something in my room."

The three girls ran upstairs to Elizabeth's tidy blue-and-white bedroom. Elizabeth opened her bureau drawer and carefully took out a tiny gold locket. On the inside of the locket was a picture of a horse. "Isn't this beautiful?" Elizabeth said softly. "This locket belonged to my mom when she was my age. She just gave it to me."

"Was that her horse?" asked Amy.

"No," Elizabeth replied. "She just liked them. She found this picture in a magazine."

"Lila may be getting a horse," Mary said.

"Really?" inquired Elizabeth. "I didn't know Lila liked horses."

"She likes them OK," said Mary. "You know how Lila is. Whatever she decides she wants, she gets."

"I wish I were getting a horse," Elizabeth said wistfully.

The front door slammed just then. "Hello," shouted Mrs. Wakefield. "Anyone home?"

Mary's face brightened. "We're up here, Mrs. Wakefield," she called.

Mrs. Wakefield stuck her head in Elizabeth's room. "Does anyone know where Jessica is?" she asked. "Her letter from Parker Smith arrived."

"He actually wrote?" said Elizabeth. "I don't believe it!"

"I'm sure Jessica is thrilled," said Mrs. Wakefield. She turned to Mary. "Have you gotten a response yet?" she asked.

"I don't think so," Mary replied. "Maybe something came in the mail today." She watched Mrs. Wakefield go back down the stairs and head toward the kitchen. "Do you need help fixing dinner?" she asked.

"I thought I'd make a salad," said Mrs. Wakefield. "You can help if you'd like." Mary and Mrs. Wakefield disappeared down the stairs.

Maybe Mary just likes to cook, Elizabeth thought. Later, though, Elizabeth noticed that Mary was also helping Mrs. Wakefield out in the garden with the weeding. *Nobody* ever helped with the weeding!

By the time Jessica got back from Lila's, Mary and Amy had gone home. "Lizzie, look!" said Jessica as she burst into her sister's room. "He actually wrote me!" She read Parker's letter out loud for the fifteenth time and then fell onto Elizabeth's bed. Suddenly, she sat straight up. "Liz, has Mom made dinner yet?" she said. "We absolutely *have* to try Parker and Vanessa's favorite recipe tonight."

"I think Mom and Mary already made something," said Elizabeth.

Jessica groaned. "Mary?" she said. "Don't tell me *she* was here today."

"She wanted to come over," Elizabeth said simply.

Jessica stared intently at her sister. "Did you watch how she follows Mom all over the place?" she said.

Elizabeth didn't answer.

"It's true, isn't it?" Jessica continued. "Mary doesn't care which one of us she comes home with. As long as she can spend time with Mom, she's happy."

"But why should it matter to you?" said Elizabeth. "You weren't even here today."

"It does matter, Lizzie," said Jessica. "I don't

happen to want to share my mother . . . especially when Mary has a perfectly good foster mother who cares about her." Jessica kicked off her shoes and lay back on the bed. "I don't want her coming over anymore," she said stiffly.

"What do you mean?" Elizabeth replied.

Jessica looked her sister straight in the eye. "I mean, I don't think either one of us should invite her over anymore," she said.

"But, Jess, that's silly," said Elizabeth. "Mary doesn't mean any harm."

Jessica's face turned red. "Liz, I don't like her here," said Jessica. "She gives me the creeps the way she hangs around Mom."

Elizabeth sighed. "All right," she said. "If it bothers you that much, I won't invite her over."

Jessica seemed relieved. "Thanks, Lizzie," she said. "I knew you would understand." She gave her sister a big hug. "And don't let Mary invite herself over, either," she added.

After Jessica left the room, Elizabeth sat quietly for a few minutes. She hoped she'd be able to discourage Mary without too much trouble. After all, Mary was such a nice girl. The last thing she wanted to do was hurt Mary's feelings. Elizabeth stared at the door that separated her room from her sister's. Even though she and Jessica were identical twins, sometimes she felt they were totally different.

Five

◇

In Mr. Bowman's classroom the next day, the staff of *The Sweet Valley Sixers* was hard at work. Career Day was only two weeks away, and there was still a lot to be done. In the corner, Julie and Caroline were busy trying to finish an advertising poster. On the other side of the room were Elizabeth and Amy. They had volunteered to coordinate the sign-up booths and were trying to make sure that each booth had the same number of participants.

Amy scanned the sign-up sheets. "How's this for original?" she said. "Every single one of the Unicorns has signed up for Gretchen Tyler."

"The Unicorns aren't big on individuality," Elizabeth said with a snicker.

"Speaking of individuality, did anyone notice Mr. Bowman's new jacket?" Julie giggled.

"Definitely Mr. B's taste," said Amy. "Terrible."

"What's wrong with red plaid?" Elizabeth said, trying to keep a straight face.

Mr. Bowman hurried through the door. "Hi, Mr. B," said Caroline loudly. "We were just talking about your new jacket."

Mr. Bowman grinned. "Do you like it?" he said. "I just bought it on sale."

Amy poked Elizabeth in the ribs.

"It's very unusual," said Caroline.

Mr. Bowman handed Elizabeth an envelope. "This just came for you," he said.

"It's from the Newspaper Guild!" said Elizabeth, ripping open the envelope.

The newspaper staff crowded around. "What does it say, Elizabeth?" said Caroline.

"'Dear Ms. Wakefield,'" Elizabeth read, "'we're pleased to announce that your paper, *The Sweet Valley Sixers*, has been chosen as a finalist in the LANG school competition.'" Elizabeth let out a loud whoop and then read on. "'To help our panel make its final decision, please submit another current issue for our judges' consideration. Congratulations and good luck. LANG.'"

"Wow," said Julie. "I don't believe it!"

"Wait till everyone hears about this," said Caroline.

"That's perfect!" said Amy. "Our next issue is Career Day."

Elizabeth was ecstatic. "Do you really think we have a chance?" she said.

"It looks like a winner to me," said Mr. Bowman.

Later, as Elizabeth hurried home to tell her

family the good news, she passed by the Altmans'. Elizabeth remembered her conversation with Jessica and quickened her step.

Just then, the Altmans' front door opened. "Hi, Elizabeth," called Mary. Elizabeth pretended she didn't hear anything and kept walking. "Elizabeth," shouted Mary. "I'm over here."

Elizabeth felt trapped. She turned and waved. "Oh, Mary," she said.

Mary ran over to the sidewalk. "Is it OK if I come over?" she asked.

"Uh, I'm not sure," said Elizabeth.

Mary looked confused.

"I have a lot of homework to do," Elizabeth explained. She pointed to her books. "Tons."

Mary seemed hurt. "OK," she said finally. "Maybe some other time."

Elizabeth nodded and then scurried on. Saying no to Mary wasn't going to be easy.

The next day, when Mary invited herself over, Elizabeth was better prepared. "Oh, wow," she said. "I can't today. The paper's been chosen as a finalist, and I've got so much preparing to do."

This time the hurt in Mary's eyes was unmistakable. "That's wonderful, Elizabeth," she said softly. "I hope you win."

Elizabeth felt awful. It seemed so mean to deprive Mary of something that obviously made her happy.

Two days later, when Mary approached Elizabeth for the third time, Elizabeth found herself feeling resentful of the position Jessica had put her in. It was obviously upsetting to Mary not to be invited over, and yet she continued to ask. Maybe it would be better for Elizabeth just to be truthful.

As Mary walked over, Elizabeth could tell that she already knew the answer. "Hi, Elizabeth," she said. There was an uncomfortable silence. "Is it OK for me to come to your house?" she asked.

Elizabeth sighed. "No, Mary, you can't," she said. Elizabeth took a deep breath. "And I'll tell you why," she continued. "Jessica's noticed that whenever you come over to our house, you only want to spend time with our mother."

Mary's face turned red. "That's not true," she said.

"I've noticed it too, Mary. You always seem to be following our mom around," said Elizabeth.

Mary's eyes filled with tears. "I've got to be going," she said. She quickly turned and rushed off.

Poor Mary. Now Elizabeth *really* felt bad. She had hoped to get some sort of honest answer from Mary, but she'd only upset her friend more.

For the next several days, every time Elizabeth saw Mary, Mary looked terribly unhappy. Finally, Elizabeth couldn't stand it any longer. Maybe she could persuade Jessica to change her mind. After all, Mary wasn't hurting anyone.

That evening, Elizabeth knocked on Jessica's door.

Jessica was busy trying on clothes in front of the mirror. "Which sweater do you think goes better with this skirt?" she asked her sister.

"The purple one," said Elizabeth.

Jessica held up the sweaters. "But they're both purple," she said.

"I know," said Elizabeth. "They both go."

"Not necessarily," said Jessica. She tossed the sweaters onto a pile on the floor. "The colors need to blend correctly. I bet Gretchen Tyler would know right away which sweater to wear."

"I saw Mary in the hall today," said Elizabeth, changing the subject. "She seems really unhappy."

"I hadn't noticed," said Jessica.

Elizabeth watched her sister slip on a familiar blouse. "Hey! That's mine!" she said.

Jessica looked down. "Oops, you're right," she said. She gave Elizabeth a sheepish look. "You don't care if I borrow it, do you?"

Elizabeth sighed. "I guess not," she said. "Jess, I think you should reconsider about Mary. She's not doing any harm by being here, and it would make her feel so much happier."

"No," said Jessica firmly. "I don't want her to come over."

"But she's miserable," Elizabeth said.

"I don't care," Jessica said stubbornly.

Elizabeth could see that it was hopeless. "OK," she finally said. "If that's the way you want it."

For the next few days, Mary avoided Jessica and Elizabeth. If she noticed either one, she would cross the hall or lower her eyes and duck into a classroom. Elizabeth still felt bad, but Mary's weird behavior only seemed to confirm what Jessica had said about her.

On Friday, Jessica attended a special meeting of the Unicorns to discuss the progress of the cookbook. As she slid into her seat, Jessica noticed Mary sitting alone by the door. Although Jessica would never admit it to anyone, she suddenly realized she felt sorry for Mary, too.

Janet clapped her hands. "Attention, everyone," she said. "I think we've heard from a good percentage of celebrities and it's time to start putting the cookbook together." The Unicorns all nodded. "I'd like to have them on sale in two weeks," Janet continued. She looked at Jessica. "Will you be able to type up the recipes by next week?"

"Uh, sure," said Jessica. She'd forgotten all about volunteering her typing services. She hoped Elizabeth would be around to help her.

"Did everyone have a chance to sign up for Gretchen Tyler for Career Day?" interrupted Tamara Chase.

Jessica grimaced. She'd forgotten that Monday was Career Day! That meant Elizabeth would be busy all week, writing the next edition of the newspaper.

"Speaking of Gretchen Tyler, has anyone seen Diana Diamond's new music video?" said Betsy. "Sweet Valley Fashions has the exact same dress that she wears in the video."

"Gretchen has such good taste." Ellen sighed.

Jessica smiled weakly. Right now, she had more important matters to think about. How was she going to get those recipes typed? She glanced at Mary. If only she and Mary were friends again!

Mary would be able to type the cookbook in no time at all!

The Unicorns finished up their meeting quickly. As Jessica headed out the door, she was surprised to see Mary approach her. "Can I talk to you for a minute?" Mary asked.

"I guess so," Jessica replied.

Mary handed Jessica a small, brightly wrapped package. "I wanted you to have this," she said.

"What is it?" said Jessica.

"Open it," Mary replied.

Jessica tore off the wrapping paper. "Mary!" she gasped. "It's your gold and silver bracelet!"

"I'm sorry for any misunderstanding," Mary said. "I'd like to be friends again."

Jessica slid the bracelet onto her arm. "It's so beautiful!" she said. She watched the light catch the intricately engraved pattern. "I've always loved this bracelet," she said happily.

"I know," said Mary.

Jessica didn't have to spend much time considering Mary's offer. Besides, now that she and Mary had made up, maybe Mary could help her type up those recipes for the Unicorns.

Mary and Jessica walked outside together. "Nancy's making zucchini soup and homemade bread for dinner tonight," said Mary. "Would you like to come over?"

Jessica grinned. "OK," she said. "I'd like that a lot."

*   *   *

When Elizabeth got home from school, she was surprised to hear that Jessica had gone to Mary's for dinner. Obviously, the two girls had made up. Elizabeth was curious to learn more.

When Jessica got home, she found Elizabeth reading in the living room. "Hi, Liz," she said.

Elizabeth sat up. "Jessica!" she replied. "What happened between you and Mary?"

"We made up," Jessica replied simply.

"But I thought you had decided never to invite Mary over again," Elizabeth said.

"I changed my mind," Jessica said. She casually held out her wrist. "Look what Mary gave me," she said.

"Jess, it's the bracelet that you love!" Elizabeth exclaimed.

Jessica slid the bracelet off her arm. "It's a token of my friendship with Mary," she said.

"So you've made up?" said Elizabeth.

"Completely," Jessica replied.

Monday was Career Day, the big day that Elizabeth had been planning for so long. As Elizabeth hurried down to breakfast that morning, she could hear Jessica frantically calling to her.

"What is it?" said Elizabeth, poking her head inside Jessica's room.

"I've lost my beige sandals," said Jessica in a desperate voice.

"I'm sure they're somewhere in your closet," Elizabeth said.

"I've looked," Jessica replied. "They're not

there." She stared at Elizabeth's feet. "May I borrow yours?" she said.

"But I'm wearing them," said Elizabeth.

"You can wear your navy ones," Jessica said. "Navy goes better with what you have on anyway."

"I happen to like these," Elizabeth grumbled.

"Liz, please," begged Jessica. "I've been planning this outfit for weeks. I want to look really fabulous when I meet Gretchen Tyler."

Elizabeth smiled. So that was it! "OK." She sighed, slipping off her shoes. "But you'd better not scuff them up. They're brand new!"

"I promise I won't, Lizzie," said Jessica. "Thanks a million."

The rest of the day flew by for Elizabeth. Even though most of the school had regular classes scheduled for the morning, Elizabeth, Amy, Julie, and Caroline were excused in order to set up the cafeteria.

After lunch, there was an opening assembly, followed by several panel discussions. After that, the student body divided into groups to meet with the career people they had signed up for.

During all this, Elizabeth took careful notes. Because this edition of the newspaper was being entered in the competition, it was especially important that she get everything right. One mistake or carelessly written article could cause the paper to lose the contest.

Elizabeth's last stop of the day was Gretchen Tyler. She carefully sneaked into the back of the room where Gretchen was speaking and took out her notebook. In front of her, the Unicorns listened to Gretchen with rapt attention. Elizabeth noticed Mary and Jessica sitting side by side in the corner. "The trick to good fashion planning is being able to catch the consumer's eye," Gretchen was saying.

This was certainly true in Gretchen's case, thought Elizabeth. She had on strange-looking webbed tights, bright-orange shoes, several layers of colorful socks, and a large baggy type of over-blouse. Gretchen's outfit was certainly "eye-catching."

Elizabeth recorded Gretchen's observations, described her strange outfit, and then yawned. She was not that interested in clothing. Good thing she was sitting in the back. Jessica would have died if she'd seen Elizabeth yawn like that.

Gretchen finally finished talking and the Unicorns applauded wildly. "Wasn't she fabulous, Lizzie?" said Jessica as she left the room.

"Unbelievable." Elizabeth grinned. She packed up her notebook and got ready to go home. This was going to be one very busy week.

Six

◇

Jessica and Mary were sitting in Jessica's room, examining the stack of recipes to be typed. "Do you think you can handle this?" Jessica asked anxiously.

"It's a lot of work," Mary admitted. Some of the celebrities had sent in three or four recipes, and then there were recipes that the girls found in places like the local newspaper and fan magazines.

"Did you see this recipe for Tuna Delight?" said Jessica. "Totally disgusting. I think we should just leave it out. It doesn't do anything for Cole Derek's reputation."

"It sounds like something he got from his grandmother." Mary giggled. "I mean, can you picture Cole Derek eating a tuna casserole made with mushroom soup and processed cheese?"

Jessica rolled over onto her back and clutched her stomach. "Yuck," she said.

Jessica heard the front door slam. "Hello. Anyone home?" called Mrs. Wakefield.

Jessica looked at Mary. "We're upstairs, Mom," she called. Jessica noticed that ever since she and Mary had made up, Mary had been very different around Mrs. Wakefield. She no longer followed Mrs. Wakefield around the kitchen or helped with the cooking.

"Elizabeth still at school?" said Mrs. Wakefield, poking her head into Jessica's room.

"I think she went to Amy's," Jessica replied.

"Did you see the final ditto master of the paper?" asked Mrs. Wakefield. "Elizabeth said she left it on the kitchen table for us to look at. She did a great job."

"So that's what's in that yellow envelope," Jessica said. "Come on, Mary. Let's go check it out."

The two girls raced downstairs. "You want anything to drink first?" Jessica asked.

"What have you got?" said Mary. She and Jessica started to dig through the shelves.

"Steven must have finished off the soda," Jessica grumbled. "What a pig." She stuck her hand into the back. "Grape juice," she said. "Want some?"

"Sure," said Mary.

Jessica poured two glasses and then handed the yellow envelope to Mary. The girls walked back upstairs and cleared some more space on Jessica's floor.

Jessica eagerly opened the envelope. "Look!"

she pointed. "Here's the story about Gretchen Tyler."

"What does it say?" said Mary.

"Listen to this headline," Jessica said. "'Fashion Consultant Addresses Enthusiastic Audience.'" She quickly skimmed through the article.

"Does it mention her outfit?" said Mary, crowding close.

Jessica hopped up. "Did you *believe* that outfit?" she said. She grabbed one of Elizabeth's beige sandals to use as a microphone and began dancing around the room and singing the new Diana Diamond hit single. "You're my one. You're my only."

Mary shrieked with laughter. "More, more," she shouted.

In a burst of inspiration, Jessica slid onto her knees just as she'd seen Diana do in the video.

"Watch out for the grape juice!" Mary gasped. It was too late. The nearly full glasses tumbled across the newspaper master.

"Quick, paper towels," shouted Jessica. She rushed into the kitchen and returned a moment later with a roll. The two girls frantically tried to mop up the mess.

"Everything's smearing," said Mary. "It's impossible to read." She and Jessica continued to blot furiously.

"Is it any better now?" said Jessica.

The two girls peered at the soggy ditto master. "Almost the whole article about Gretchen has been ruined, not to mention your floor," said Mary.

Jessica couldn't believe it. "We have to do something," she said. "Elizabeth's going to kill us."

Mary took a deep breath. "Maybe we should just tell her and get it over with," she said.

Jessica remembered the mix-up she'd almost caused in the last edition. "Impossible," she said. She held up the paper. "Maybe we can fix it instead."

"But we don't know what she wrote," Mary said.

Jessica looked down at the paper. "The only story that's been ruined is the one about Gretchen," she said. "We'll just fill in the missing paragraphs and then you can retype it on the extra ditto masters we have for the cookbook."

Mary looked doubtful.

"We were there, weren't we?" said Jessica. "Don't worry. No one's going to notice a few paragraphs."

Jessica set to work. The first part of the article was still readable. "I'm not sure I like this headline." Jessica frowned. "Don't you think it would sound better this way: 'Fabulous Gretchen Tyler Speaks to the Unicorns'?"

"I don't know, Jessica," said Mary. "If Elizabeth had wanted it that way, she would have written it like that."

Jessica picked up a piece of paper. "But my way sounds much better," she said. She wrote down the headline the way she wanted it and then scanned the first two paragraphs. "This first part looks fine," she said. Jessica strained her eyes.

"But the next part is gone. Something about what she was wearing." She looked at Mary and smiled. "How's this?" she said. "Gretchen was wearing these incredible-looking Spandex tights with layers 'n' layers of Day-Glo socks."

"Layers 'n' layers?" said Mary.

Jessica ignored Mary's comment. "How do you spell incredible?" she asked.

"I-N-C-R-E-D-D-A-B-L-E," said Mary.

The next few sentences were a breeze. Jessica couldn't believe how easy it was to write. After she finished the article, Mary retyped the page.

"It looks like we're still about one paragraph short," Mary said.

Jessica glanced at the pile of recipes. "Here," she said. "Let's include Parker Smith's recipe for sweet 'n' sour barbecued ribs."

Mary fit the recipe onto the bottom of the page. "I hope Elizabeth likes this." She sighed.

"It looks great," said Jessica. "I can't believe how well it turned out." Even though Jessica had made more changes than she'd planned, she knew Elizabeth would forgive her once she saw what a great job she'd done. No one could even tell that Gretchen's article had been rewritten. And including the recipe was a stroke of genius!

Jessica put the newspaper back into the yellow envelope. "I'm going to put this on the kitchen table," she told Mary. "You can get started on the recipes if you want."

When Jessica got back, Mary had disappeared. "Mary, where are you?" Jessica called.

Mary poked her head out of Mrs. Wakefield's

room. "I was just talking to your mother about the cookbook," she said.

Jessica's stomach tightened. Maybe Mary wasn't over her mother after all. "We still have a lot of work to do," Jessica said stiffly. "We haven't even begun typing the recipes."

"I know," said Mary. "Gotta go, Mrs. Wakefield," she said. Mary quietly returned to Jessica's room. For a moment, there was an uncomfortable silence. Mary handed the recipes to Jessica. "Why don't you read them to me, and I'll type?" she said.

"OK," Jessica replied. "Let's start with Jeremy Frank's lemon-lime pie." Before long, both girls were absorbed in the project, and Jessica had forgotten about her doubts, at least for the moment.

Later that evening, Jessica was on her way to Elizabeth's room to return her shoes when she overheard her parents talking.

"I had a call from Nancy Altman today," said Mr. Wakefield. Jessica stopped walking and strained her ears. "It seems that she and Tom are interested in adopting Mary," he said. "She wanted to know more about the legal procedure."

"Really, Ned?" said Mrs. Wakefield. "That's wonderful. Mary's such a nice girl."

Jessica tried to get closer, but the voices faded out. No matter, thought Jessica. The news about Mary was perfect. If Mary had a mother of her very own, she'd leave Jessica's mother alone. What could be better? Jessica hurried off to tell Elizabeth.

Elizabeth sat hunched at her desk, trying to

solve a difficult math problem. She'd spent so much extra time on the paper recently, that she'd fallen behind in her classes. Math was the worst, too. When a student missed a day or two of math, it could take weeks to catch up.

Elizabeth heard a knock at the door. "Come in," she said.

Jessica placed the beige sandals on Elizabeth's desk and grinned. "Didn't I tell you I'd take good care of them?" she said.

Elizabeth stared at the shoes. "Jess! You polished them!" she said.

"Of course," Jessica replied. She hoped Elizabeth wouldn't notice the tiny spot of grape juice on the back of the right heel. She'd managed to cover the rest up with the shoe polish.

Jessica remembered her good news. "Liz, guess what?" she said. "I just heard Mom and Dad talking. Dad said that the Altmans want to adopt Mary."

"Really?" said Elizabeth. "That's great! Mary will finally have her own mother."

"Wait till I tell Lila and Ellen," said Jessica. "Maybe we can throw Mary an adoption party or something."

Elizabeth paused. "Jess," she said, "maybe you should wait before you tell anyone. What if it doesn't work out or something?"

"Why shouldn't it work out?" said Jessica. "The Altmans will make perfect parents."

"But maybe Mary wants to tell everyone herself," said Elizabeth.

Jessica shrugged. "I don't see why," she said.

"Besides, she can't possibly spread the word to everyone all by herself."

Elizabeth didn't answer. "So how's the paper?" Jessica asked, changing the subject. "Did you notice that Mary and I put your typewriter back in your room?"

"Is this the new Jessica Wakefield?" Elizabeth laughed. "First you polish my shoes, and then you actually return my typewriter before I have to ask you to dig it out of your room."

Jessica smiled modestly. "Mary and I read the newspaper," she said. "We really liked it."

Elizabeth beamed. "You're not just saying that?"

Jessica shook her head. "I thought it was great," she said. "When does it get run off?" she added.

"Tomorrow morning," said Elizabeth.

"I can't wait to see it," said Jessica.

That night, as Jessica lay in bed, she thought some more about her parents' conversation. Mary had probably been waiting a long time for someone to adopt her. This was no doubt the best thing that had ever happened to her. Suddenly, Jessica sat straight up. She'd just thought of a brilliant way to spread the news!

She put on her robe and slippers. Quietly she slipped out of her bedroom and down the stairs. Sitting on the kitchen table was Elizabeth's yellow envelope.

Jessica carefully removed the masters and spread them out. Using her neatest handwriting, at the very bottom of Caroline Pearce's gossip column, Jessica added this sentence: "This just in! Mary Giaccio, Sweet Valley's most popular foster girl, is about to be adopted!"

With a satisfied smile, Jessica put the ditto master back in the envelope and left it on the kitchen table. Having the newspaper there had turned out to be a stroke of luck. Jessica couldn't wait to see Mary's face when she read the good news!

Seven

◇

Elizabeth combed her hair back and fastened it with a pretty green barrette that accented her turquoise eyes. From her bureau drawer, she carefully took out the gold locket and clasped it around her neck. Today was the day the newspaper came out, and Elizabeth wanted to look her prettiest. After she slipped on her favorite skirt and sweater and applied a tiny bit of clear lip gloss to her mouth, she walked confidently down to the kitchen.

"Don't you look pretty today!" exclaimed Mrs. Wakefield.

Elizabeth slid into her chair and took a sip of orange juice. "Thank you," she replied.

Steven looked up from his bowl of cereal. "What's the occasion?" he asked.

"I just felt like getting dressed up for a change," Elizabeth said.

Jessica burst into the kitchen. "Ta-da!" she said. She spun around in a graceful pirouette to show off her four pairs of socks, layered one on top of the other, just as Gretchen Tyler's had been.

"Another beauty queen," Steven muttered.

"What's for breakfast, Mom?" said Jessica. "I'm starved."

Mrs. Wakefield handed Jessica a box of cereal. "Self-service," she said. She glanced at her watch. Gotta go, kids. I've got an early appointment, and I'm already late. Last one out, lock up." She hurried out the door.

"So much for scrambled eggs," Jessica grumbled.

Elizabeth took her cereal bowl to the sink and picked up the yellow envelope.

"You leaving?" said Jessica. "Wait up." She gulped down a few spoonfuls of cereal and tossed the rest into the garbage. "We haven't walked to school together in ages." She grinned.

The twins looked at Steven, who was pouring another bowl of cereal. "Last one out, lock up," they chorused.

All the way to school, Jessica and Elizabeth joked and laughed about everything they could think of. Elizabeth couldn't remember the last time she'd had so much fun with her twin.

When the girls got to school, Elizabeth headed for Mr. Bowman's room.

"Would you like me to take that?" Jessica offered. "It's on my way."

Elizabeth handed the envelope to Jessica. "Thanks, Jess," she said. "You've been awfully nice recently."

Jessica merely smiled. She couldn't wait until *The Sweet Valley Sixers* came out later that afternoon!

After Jessica turned in the newspaper, she rushed off to show Janet the typed-up cookbook recipes before the bell rang. As Janet flipped through the pages, Jessica could tell she was impressed. "I love how you arranged these," said Janet. "It almost looks professional."

"I had a little help from Mary," Jessica said. She noticed that Janet was also wearing several layers of socks.

Janet pointed to Jessica's wrist. "That bracelet looks familiar. Doesn't Mary have one just like it?" she asked.

"It was a gift from Mary," Jessica replied. "It's a token of our friendship." Jessica couldn't contain her secret any longer. "Janet, there will be a special announcement about Mary in Caroline's gossip column today," she said.

Janet looked skeptical. "Are you sure?" she said. "Caroline never gets anything right."

"But *I* wrote this," Jessica said.

Janet leaned forward. "What is it?" she said. "Tell me!"

Jessica shook her head. "You'll find out soon enough," she teased. She grabbed her books and stood up. "All I can say for now is that it's very, very good news."

After lunch, Amy, Julie, and Caroline met in Mr. Bowman's room to staple newspapers. "Check this out!" said Caroline. She pointed to her gossip column. "Mary Giaccio is getting adopted. Elizabeth must have added this at the last minute."

"That's great!" said Amy. "The Altmans are really nice."

Julie scanned the first page. "Elizabeth must have put in this recipe for barbecued ribs, too," she said.

Amy frowned. "What do barbecued ribs have to do with Career Day?" she said.

Julie shrugged. "I don't know," she said. "Maybe something to do with a career as a cook?"

"Hi, Mr. Bowman," said Caroline. "Did you hear Mary Giaccio's going to be adopted?"

"Is this a *confirmed* rumor, Caroline?" He grinned.

"According to Elizabeth it is," Caroline said.

"In that case, I'll believe it," said Mr. Bowman. "How are those newspapers coming?"

Amy handed Mr. Bowman a copy. "Hot off the press," she announced.

Mr. Bowman opened the paper to page two and quickly looked it over. "Who covered Gretchen Tyler?" he asked.

"I think Elizabeth did," said Julie. "Why?"

"I see some spelling errors," he said. He skimmed the story. "Not a bad article, though." He smiled. " A little livelier than usual. I'm not quite sure I understand the recipe."

"Neither does anyone else," said Amy. She picked up a stack of newspapers. "I'll drop these off on my way to math," she said.

Amy spotted Elizabeth forty minutes later as she walked out of Ms. Wyler's room.

"How did everything go?" asked Elizabeth.

"Great," said Amy. "The paper looks really good. That's nice news about Mary, too. Everyone is glad to hear it."

"What news?" said Elizabeth.

"The news you wrote at the bottom of Caroline's column," said Amy. Elizabeth looked confused. "About Mary being adopted," Amy explained.

Elizabeth gasped. "But . . ."

"I wasn't too sure about the recipe for sweet 'n' sour barbecued ribs, though," Amy continued. "What does that have to do with Career Day?"

Elizabeth was horrified. Obviously, someone had been tampering with the paper. And Elizabeth had a very strong suspicion of who it was. "Amy, may I please see a copy of the paper?" she said, trying to stay calm.

"Is something the matter?" asked Amy.

When Elizabeth spotted her sister's handwriting, her suspicions were confirmed. Then she noticed the article about Gretchen Tyler. "Have all the newspapers been distributed?" she asked.

Amy nodded. "What's going on?" she asked.

"Excuse me," Elizabeth replied grimly. "I have to go wring someone's neck."

At the other end of school, Mary was leaving study hall when she was approached by Lila, Janet, and Tamara. "Congratulations, Mary!" they all said.

"What for?" Mary replied.

Janet smiled. "Mrs. Altman will make a wonderful mother," she said. "We're all *very* excited for you."

Mary turned pale. "Nancy isn't my mother," she said.

"Not yet, she isn't," said Janet. "But according to this, she will be soon." Janet waved the paper in Mary's face and pointed to Caroline's column.

Mary stared at the paper.

"It's true, isn't it?" said Tamara. "You *are* going to get the Altmans to adopt you?"

"I—I don't know what you're talking about," Mary stammered. "My mother is . . ." Her eyes filled with tears. "Excuse me," she said. She rushed away before she finished her sentence.

"That's weird," said Janet. "You'd think she'd be grateful somebody wanted her."

"You never know about Mary," Lila said. The girls shook their heads sadly.

Elizabeth walked through the halls with a determined step. Where had Jessica disappeared to? She spotted Lila, Janet, and Tamara on their way out of the building. "Have you seen Jessica?" she asked them.

Lila shook her head. "Not since this morning," she replied.

Elizabeth scanned the hall.

"Mary might know where she is," Lila added. "I wouldn't bother her right now, though."

"Why?" said Elizabeth. "Is she upset?"

Lila shrugged. "I guess so," she said. "I don't

know why, though. All we did was congratulate her."

"Which way did she go?" said Elizabeth.

Janet pointed to the door.

Elizabeth hurried off. Poor Mary. Jessica had no right to print such personal information without first asking her friend. She spotted Mary on the other side of the parking lot.

"Mary, wait!" called Elizabeth.

Mary quickened her step.

Elizabeth ran to catch up. "Mary, please wait," she said. "I want to talk to you."

Mary spun around angrily. "What is it?" she said. "Do you want to congratulate me, too?"

"Mary, I'm sorry," Elizabeth said. "I told Jessica she should wait before she told everyone your news."

Mary stopped. "*Jessica* wrote that?" she said.

Elizabeth slowly nodded.

Mary's eyes filled with tears again. "But I thought Jessica was my friend," she said.

"She is," Elizabeth replied. "She just wanted to be the first one to tell everyone your good news. She didn't mean anything bad."

"Good news?" said Mary sadly. She began to cry softly. "What's so good about it?"

"But don't you want the Altmans to adopt you?" said Elizabeth. "Don't you want a mother of your very own?"

"I *have* a mother of my very own," Mary replied fiercely.

Elizabeth was shocked. She'd always assumed that Mary had no parents. "Where is she, then?" she asked.

Mary's shoulders slouched over. "I don't know," she replied sadly. She looked Elizabeth straight in the eye. "But she's looking for me right now. I know she is."

"I don't understand," said Elizabeth.

Mary's voice quivered. "Sh—she's . . ."

"You can tell me what happened," said Elizabeth gently. "I promise I won't tell anyone."

Mary sighed deeply. "When I was four years old," she began, "my parents got a divorce. We were living in Baltimore at the time, and Mom decided we should move to California. One day she packed up everything we owned in the car and we just drove off. We made it as far as Kansas, and then we ran out of money. That's when Mom met Annie."

Mary's voice shuddered.

"Mom got a job at a restaurant, and Annie was one of the other waitresses," she explained. "I never really liked her. She used to sometimes baby-sit for me when Mom had to work late. Anyway, after we'd been there for about six months, my grandmother in Florida got very sick. My mom had to go take care of her for a while." Mary's eyes filled with tears again. "Mom left me with Annie, and that's . . ." Mary paused to wipe away a tear. ". . . that's the last time I ever saw my mother," she said sadly.

Elizabeth felt awful. "What happened to her?" she said.

Mary took out a tissue and blew her nose. "Annie told me that she died," she said. She looked up. "But I've never really believed that. I know my mom is out there somewhere, and she's looking for me. That's why . . ." Her eyes brimmed with more tears. ". . . I could never let anyone adopt me."

"But what happened to Annie?" said Elizabeth.

"Shortly after my mother left, Annie brought me to California, but I guess I wasn't too much fun for her," Mary said. "We were living in this tiny little room with no money, and it seemed like Annie was always working. She used to leave me with her neighbor for days at a time. I hated it. One day she left for work, and she never came back."

Elizabeth's eyes widened. "You mean she abandoned you?" she said.

"I guess you could call it that." Mary shrugged. "Then a really nice lady from the welfare department came and got me, and took me to this children's home. It wasn't long before they'd found me a foster home, the first of many."

Elizabeth nodded sympathetically. "Did you like any of the foster homes?" she asked.

"Some more than others," Mary answered. "I especially like the Altmans," she added. "But I still think about my mother all the time. Sometimes I dream about her, and she always tells me to wait— that she'll be back to get me one day."

Elizabeth wished there were some way she

could help Mary. Maybe Mary shouldn't lose this opportunity to have a real home.

The two girls stopped in front of the Altmans' house.

"Mary, don't you think you should change your mind?" said Elizabeth gently. "Maybe you won't ever have a chance like this again."

Mary shook her head. "No," she said firmly. "I've made up my mind. I'm going to wait for my real mother . . . and if she doesn't find me by the time I grow up, then I'll go and look for her." She stared at the Altmans' front door. "I told Nancy and Tom that I'd give them my answer this afternoon," she said. "They're going to be really disappointed."

"Would you like me to come with you?" said Elizabeth.

Mary shook her head sadly. "No," she said. "This is something I have to do by myself." She smiled at Elizabeth. "Thanks for listening to me, though," she said. "I feel much better now that I've talked to someone."

Mary turned and started up the front walk.

"Mary?" said Elizabeth. Mary turned back around. "If you want to talk to someone later, call me," she said.

Mary grinned. "Thanks, Elizabeth," she replied. "I will."

Eight

◇

Twenty minutes later, Jessica burst through the door of the Wakefields' house. "I'm home," she yelled.

The house was silent. "Liz, are you here?" shouted Jessica.

Out in the backyard, Elizabeth sat quietly in her favorite spot, "the thinking seat." The low branch of the old pine tree was where Elizabeth liked to go whenever she wanted to be alone with her thoughts.

Elizabeth heard Jessica's calls but wasn't sure she should respond. She still hadn't decided what she wanted to say to her sister. At first, she was angry with Jessica for being so thoughtless. But her conversation with Mary had forced her to calm down and think about everything. She and Jessica had so much to be thankful for!

"There you are!" said Jessica. She pushed her

way through the branches. "You wouldn't believe what happened to me on the way home."

"Jess," said Elizabeth, "why don't you save it for another time?"

Jessica looked hurt. "Did I do something wrong?" she asked.

Elizabeth sighed. "I had a long talk with Mary this afternoon. She was very upset about what you did."

Jessica looked genuinely surprised. "Why?" she said.

"Because Mary doesn't want to be adopted," Elizabeth replied. She explained how Mary was hoping that her real mother might one day find her.

Jessica sat down next to her sister. "Poor Mary," she said. "I didn't mean anything bad."

"I know you didn't," Elizabeth said. "You just didn't think." The two girls sat quietly for a few minutes. "Jess," said Elizabeth, "there's something else we need to talk about. Why did you rewrite my story about Gretchen Tyler and add a recipe at the bottom?"

"Did you like it?" said Jessica brightly. "When Mary and I were working on the cookbooks I accidentally spilled a little grape juice on your original so I had to fix it."

"But this is the issue I'm submitting to the newspaper competition," Elizabeth said. "I can't turn it in like this. The whole thing will have to be redone. It's full of spelling errors, and it has this ridiculous recipe."

"That happens to be Parker Smith's personal barbecue recipe," Jessica replied in a huffy voice. "I thought it was a good idea."

"It wasn't," Elizabeth said. She could feel herself getting angry again. "What gives you the right to change someone's work, anyway?" she said. "Did you ever stop to think that maybe I might not like what you did? Or that I might look like a fool in front of my friends or Mr. Bowman? Did you even ask me if you could do that?"

Jessica's eyes narrowed. "I wouldn't be so critical if I were you," she said. "You should be happy I tried to fix your story. It sounds much better now."

"I never wanted it fixed in the first place," said Elizabeth. She stood up angrily. "Next time you decide to do someone a favor, Jess," she said, "make sure it's not me." She ran inside and slammed the door.

Jessica sat back down with a thud. Her sister had some nerve! How was that for gratitude? She kicked the tree trunk and frowned.

Several doors away, Mary sat nervously in the Altmans' living room. Next to her on the couch were Tom and Nancy Altman. Mary cleared her throat.

"I've been giving a lot of thought to your offer," she began. "And I know you'd like to have an answer soon." She looked down and fumbled with her ring. She knew how disappointed the Altmans would be.

Mary paused. "I want you to know that you're the nicest foster parents I've ever had," she continued. "I really mean that." Mary looked up. "But I can't accept," she said. "I'm still hoping my real mother is alive and that she'll find me."

Mr. Altman squeezed his wife's hand. "Mary," he said gently, "it's been seven and a half years since you've seen your mother. Don't you think if she were alive she'd have found you by now?"

Mary shook her head stubbornly. "Not necessarily," she said.

Mrs. Altman looked at her husband. "Mary, dear," she said, "even the welfare agency agrees that the chances of your mother being alive are very, very slim."

Mary thrust out her chin. "It's not true," she said. "I don't believe it."

Mrs. Altman sighed and leaned back on the sofa.

"Won't you reconsider?" said Mr. Altman. "It would mean so much to Nancy and me to have you as our daughter."

Tears filled Mary's eyes. "I can't," she said. "As much as I care for you both, I just can't."

Mr. Altman glanced at his wife and then took Mary's hands. "We appreciate your honesty, Mary," he said.

"And we certainly understand your feelings," added Mrs. Altman. She looked sadly at her husband. "Tom, I think we should respect Mary's decision."

Mr. Altman nodded and let go of Mary's hands. "I suppose you're right," he said.

Mrs. Altman put her arm around Mary's

shoulder. "Mary, dear, I hope you realize that we love you very much. And if you should change your mind, we'll be here for you."

Mary breathed a sigh of relief and then reached over and gave Mrs. Altman a hug. "Thank you for understanding," she whispered. "And I won't forget your offer. It's the nicest offer anyone has ever given me."

For the next several days, Elizabeth and Jessica hardly spoke to each other. To make matters worse, Jessica apologized to Mary, so Mary and Jessica were friends again. Elizabeth felt as if somehow she'd come out on the wrong end of everything. It didn't seem fair.

The worst part, though, happened when Elizabeth turned in the story about Gretchen Tyler. She had spent several hours trying to reconstruct the story as she'd written it.

"What's this?" Mr. Bowman frowned.

"I redid the story on Gretchen Tyler," Elizabeth explained. "I realized there were some spelling errors and I also wanted to change a few other things."

Mr. Bowman quickly skimmed the article. "What was wrong with the first version?" he said.

"It was awful," Elizabeth replied.

"I kind of liked it," he said. "Aside from the spelling mistakes and the recipe at the bottom, I thought it had a nice, spunky tone."

Elizabeth couldn't believe it. How could he say that? Jessica didn't know the first thing about writing.

"Do you think you could put some of those sentences back in?" Mr. Bowman added.

"You really liked the first version better?" Elizabeth said incredulously.

"Not better," said Mr. Bowman. "I just thought it had a more fun point of view."

Elizabeth took the paper out of Mr. Bowman's hand. She turned and quickly left the room.

On the way out of the building, Elizabeth ran into Mary.

"Hi, Elizabeth," Mary said.

Elizabeth hardly looked up. "Hi," she said. She was in no mood to see Mary right now.

"Thanks for taking the time to listen to me the other day," Mary said. "It meant a lot to me."

Elizabeth nodded. "Don't mention it."

"I haven't seen you much the last few days," Mary said.

"I've been busy with the paper," Elizabeth replied dryly.

There was an uncomfortable silence. "I'm sorry you and Jessica aren't speaking," Mary said finally. "Jessica felt really bad when she spilled that grape juice on your paper. She was only trying to help."

"But that was *my* story," Elizabeth said angrily. "She had no right to change it."

"Jessica didn't mean anything," said Mary. "She was just being Jessica." She looked at Elizabeth and grinned. "After you and I talked, *I* was willing to forgive her," she said.

Elizabeth nodded. "That's a good point," she said. She sighed loudly. "Sometimes I really want to strangle Jessica. All she ever thinks about is herself."

"That's true," replied Mary, "but think how much fun she is. Don't you think it's great that she can be that way?"

Elizabeth thought about all the predicaments her sister had gotten her into. "I guess so," she said and laughed. "Jessica *can* be a lot of fun to be around. You never know what to expect."

Mary got serious. "Elizabeth," she said, "there's something I haven't told anyone yet. The welfare agency has told me that since I've chosen not to be adopted, maybe it's better that I move on. I'll be going to another foster home in Northern California at the end of the term."

"You're kidding," said Elizabeth. "What did the Altmans say when you told them?"

"They'd still like me to stay, but the welfare agency thinks it wouldn't be fair to anyone else who might be waiting to be adopted." She smiled sadly. "I'm really going to miss you and Jessica," she said. "It's always so hard to move on. I really hate it. I never know what kind of family I'll get stuck with next or what to expect. I guess the only thing that keeps me going is the hope that my real mother is still out there, looking for me."

Elizabeth squeezed her friend's hand. "Mary, I hope you find her someday. I do."

That evening, as Elizabeth sat at her desk, she thought about her conversation with Mary. It must be so tough for Mary to have to move from place to place all the time. She pulled out a copy of *The Sweet Valley Sixers* and stared at the article about

Gretchen Tyler. What had Mr. Bowman meant about Jessica's version being more "fun"? She carefully reread the story. Maybe Jessica's description about what Gretchen was wearing *was* a little more colorful than her own, Elizabeth thought. She took out a pencil and put the sentence back in. Elizabeth looked at the next sentence with a practiced eye. Jessica had the right idea. The words just needed to be rearranged.

Before long, the article had been transformed. As Elizabeth read the story one last time, she realized that she was no longer angry with Jessica. She got up from her desk and tiptoed through the bathroom that connected the girls' rooms.

Jessica was lying on her stomach on the floor. She was listening to her Walkman, doing her math homework, and practicing her leg lifts for cheerleading all at the same time. Elizabeth laughed and grabbed her sister's toe.

Jessica rolled onto her back and pulled off the earphones.

"I was wondering," Elizabeth said, "if you'd like to share that ice-cream bar that Steven hid behind the ice machine in the freezer," she asked.

Jessica smiled back. "Only," she replied with a sly grin, "if you don't tell him where I hid the rest of the box!"

Nine

◈

Elizabeth sat absorbed in a book outside Sweet Valley Middle School. She was vaguely aware of the fact that someone was calling her name.

"Elizabeth!" said Jessica. "Earth to Elizabeth!"

Elizabeth looked up with a dreamy expression on her face. "Yes, Jessica?" she said.

"I've been calling you for five minutes," said Jessica. "Didn't you hear me?"

"What's up?" asked Elizabeth. She marked her place with a bookmark.

"I wanted to show you how our cookbooks came out," said Jessica. She proudly pulled a copy out of her book bag. On the cover was a unicorn surrounded by some photos of the celebrities. "Doesn't it look fabulous?" she said. "Kimberly Haver designed it."

"It's terrific," Elizabeth said. "When do they go on sale?"

"Tomorrow," Jessica replied.

Elizabeth looked across the parking lot. "Have you seen Amy?" she asked. "I invited her over for the afternoon."

"Really?" said Jessica. "Mary's coming over too. Let's all walk home together." She sat down next to her sister on the curb.

Several minutes later, Mary came out of the building. "Hi," she said. She turned to Elizabeth. "Amy said to tell you she has to stay late for detention. Julie dared her to do a back flip in the library, and she got caught."

"Great," groaned Jessica. "Now we'll be stuck here forever."

"You go ahead," said Elizabeth. "I don't mind waiting. I've got my book."

"You sure?" said Mary.

Elizabeth smiled. She'd rather be reading her book anyway. "I'll see you later," she said.

A few minutes later Elizabeth finished the chapter and looked around for Amy. There was still no sign of her. Elizabeth scanned the parking lot. She was surprised to see her mother heading toward her from the other side of the school yard.

Elizabeth stood up and waved. "Hi, Mom," she shouted. Her mother didn't seem to notice her. "Is everything OK?" she yelled. Mrs. Wakefield continued to walk in her direction.

Elizabeth got up and ran toward her mother. Maybe something was wrong. Halfway across the parking lot, she stopped. That wasn't her mother at all! The resemblance, though, was amazing. The woman had the same blond hair and blue eyes as Mrs. Wakefield. She even wore her hair in a similar style.

The strange woman approached Elizabeth. "Hello," she said and smiled.

"Hello," said Elizabeth.

"Do you go to school here?" the woman asked.

Elizabeth looked back at the entrance to the school. "Yes," she said.

"Then you must know Mary Giaccio," the woman said.

Elizabeth relaxed. "Yes, I do," she said.

The woman looked toward the school building. "Do you think she's still in school?" she said.

"No," Elizabeth replied. "As a matter of fact, she's with my twin sister right now. They're probably at our house."

"Well, isn't that a coincidence!" said the woman. "Is there any way you can direct me there? I'm an old friend of the family."

Elizabeth hesitated. She knew Mary didn't have any real family.

The woman looked slightly flustered. "What I meant to say," she said, "is that Mary lived with our family for a while."

"Ahh!" said Elizabeth. The woman must be one of Mary's former foster parents. She looked up and saw Amy running toward them.

"Sorry I'm late, Elizabeth," she said breathlessly. "Did Mary tell you why I couldn't make it?"

Elizabeth nodded. "This is a friend of Mary's," she gestured.

"Hello," said Amy.

"I was just telling her that Mary is at our house with Jessica," Elizabeth continued. She looked at the woman and smiled. "We're going there now if you'd like to walk with us. It's not far."

"That would be very nice," said the woman. "I haven't seen Mary in a long time."

The three walked together for several minutes in silence. "Have you girls known Mary a long time?" the woman asked.

"Ever since she came to live with the Altmans," Elizabeth replied.

"Are they nice people?" said the woman.

"They're really great," Amy said. "Mrs. Altman runs a catering service."

"I hadn't heard that," said the woman. "Lucky Mary! Does she like school?"

"She's in the Unicorns," said Amy. "That's a club made up of the most popular girls in the school."

"So she's well liked?" said the woman.

"Very," said Elizabeth. "And she's not stuck-up like a lot of the other Unicorns. She's friendly with girls who aren't in the Unicorns too."

"Like us," Amy said.

The woman nodded thoughtfully. "Does she seem happy to you?"

"I think so," said Amy suspiciously. "She's pretty quiet, so you don't always know what she's thinking."

Elizabeth stared at the woman and wondered why she was here. Maybe she also wanted to adopt Mary.

"Tell me about the Altmans," said the woman. "Do they have any other children?"

"Just Mary," said Elizabeth.

"So she must be very special to them," said the woman.

They rounded the corner that led them to the Wakefields' block. "That's the Altmans' house," said Elizabeth, pointing.

"Oh!" said the woman wistfully. "What a lovely home. Mary must love living there."

"Here's our house." Elizabeth pointed. "Mary is just a few houses away."

Amy headed across the lawn. "Want me to tell Mary you're here?" she asked.

The woman froze. "No!" she said.

Elizabeth and Amy stopped. "But I thought you wanted to see her," said Amy.

"I—I'm not sure anymore," stammered the woman. "She may not remember me. It's been a long time."

Elizabeth looked at Amy. What was it about this woman that was so strange? Why was she hesitating? Elizabeth had a sudden horrible feeling. "Is your name Annie?" she demanded.

The woman turned pale. "No," she whispered.

Elizabeth gasped. Suddenly, it was all clear. "You're Mary's mother!" she said.

Tears welled up in the woman's eyes. She nodded. "I can't believe I've finally found her. All these years of searching, hoping."

Elizabeth couldn't believe it either. Mary was right. Her mother *had* been looking for her! And no wonder Mary liked to spend time with Mrs. Wakefield! She and Mary's mother looked like sisters.

"Don't you want to go inside?" said Amy.

The woman hesitated. "She's really happy here in Sweet Valley, isn't she?" she said. "Maybe it's wrong of me to try to come back into her life now that she's finally found a good home."

Elizabeth took a deep breath. Now was her chance. "I don't think so," she said.

Mary's mother and Amy looked at her in surprise.

"Mary is doing OK here, and she has friends and all that, but she's not happy," she said firmly. Elizabeth looked directly at Mary's mother. "She wishes she had her real mother back," she said.

"Are you sure?" said Mary's mother. "I thought the Altmans were going to adopt her."

Elizabeth shook her head. "The Altmans would *like* to adopt her, but Mary turned them down."

"I don't understand," said Mary's mother.

Elizabeth explained how Mary had told her that she was convinced her mother was still alive. "She even dreams about you," Elizabeth said. "And in her dream, you always tell her to wait because one day you're going to find her."

"I had no idea," Mary's mother said softly.

"It's true," said Elizabeth. "More than anything in the world, Mary wants her real mother back."

Mary's mother looked toward the Wakefield house.

"*Now* are you going inside?" said Amy.

Elizabeth took Mary's mother gently by the elbow. "Come on," she said. "Mary's been waiting for this for a long time."

Amy, Elizabeth, and Mary's mother hurried up the front walk. "I'll ring the doorbell," Amy volunteered.

Jessica and Mary were upstairs, trying on clothes in Jessica's room, when the doorbell rang. "Steven," yelled Jessica, "would you please get the door?"

Steven walked past Jessica's room. "No." He grinned. "You're just as close as I am."

"I thought you were in the kitchen," Jessica grumbled.

"*I'll* get it," said Mary.

The doorbell rang again.

"Will someone please answer the door?" Mrs. Wakefield shouted from her bedroom.

Mary hurried down the stairs. "Coming," she yelled. She pulled the door open.

"Mary?" said her mother.

Mary stood very still and stared.

"Mary, do you know who I am?" said her mother.

Mary's face slowly changed from one of uncertainty to one of recognition. "Mom?" she whispered.

Mary's mother held out her arms and Mary fell into them in a tearful heap. "Oh, Mom," she sobbed. "You've finally found me!"

Ten

◇

Jessica was aware of a lot of commotion in the front hall. "What's going on?" she yelled. When she didn't get an answer, she looked down the stairs. At first, she thought she saw her mother hug Mary. Then she saw Elizabeth hug Mary, Mary hug Amy, and Amy hug Elizabeth. Jessica became even more confused when her real mother emerged from the bedroom.

"Is someone here?" asked Mrs. Wakefield, coming to the top of the stairs.

Elizabeth signaled to her mother and Jessica. "Mom, Jessica," she said, "I'd like you to meet Mary's mother—her *real* mother."

Jessica did a double take. "Are you serious?" she said.

Mary's mother put out her hand. "Andrea Robinson," she replied. "You must be Elizabeth's twin."

Mrs. Wakefield was amazed. "I wasn't aware that Mary had a mother," she said.

Mrs. Robinson looked at her daughter and smiled. "Mary was taken from me seven and a half years ago," she said. "I've been looking for her ever since."

"You mean she was kidnapped?" asked Amy.

Mrs. Robinson nodded and gave Mary another hug. "It's all behind us now," she said.

There was an awkward pause in the conversation. Mrs. Robinson and Mary looked as though they were going to start crying again.

"Why don't we all go inside?" said Mrs. Wakefield. "It sounds as if Mary and her mother have quite a lot of talking to do."

Mary stuck close to her mother as Mrs. Wakefield led the group into the living room. "I can't believe how much you've grown," her mother told her. "You've turned into such a beautiful young woman." Mrs. Robinson's eyes misted over with tears again as she looked around the room. "You don't know how much it means to me to finally find my daughter," she said. "All those years of searching and never knowing if I'd ever succeed." She reached over and squeezed Mary's hand.

"Can I get you anything?" asked Mrs. Wakefield.

"Not right now," said Mrs. Robinson. She leaned back on the couch.

"Mrs. Robinson, how did you ever manage to find Mary?" said Elizabeth.

Mary's mother took a deep breath. "It wasn't easy," she said. She began by telling everyone the part that Elizabeth already knew—how she decided to take Mary to California after her divorce and how she ran out of money in Kansas. When she got to the part about leaving Mary with Annie, Mary sat up stiffly.

"My mother had been ill for a long time," said Mrs. Robinson. "When I got a call that she was in the hospital, I felt it was important for me to be there. Annie had watched Mary before, and so I didn't think she'd mind helping me out in an emergency like this. In fact, Annie was always talking about how she wanted a little girl of her very own. Had I known what she had in mind, I never would have trusted Mary with her. About a week after I left, my mother died. It took me another week to get her affairs in order. All the time, though, I was in regular touch with Annie and Mary." She looked at her daughter. "Do you remember your favorite doll?" she asked. "You called her Huggums."

Mary nodded. "I think so," she said.

"The last time I called, you told me on the phone that Huggums had broken her arm and that I'd better hurry home." She looked at her daughter sadly. "That was the last time we ever spoke. When I returned several days later you and Annie were gone."

The room was quiet.

"What did you do?" asked Amy. "Did you call the police?"

"Of course," said Mrs. Robinson. "But by then, several days had gone by. The police put out all sorts of bulletins, but they weren't very encouraging. This is a big country, and Annie could have gone anywhere. I was frantic. I kept thinking how frightened Mary must be. What did Annie tell her had happened to her mommy? Was she being properly cared for and loved? My heart ached for her."

"What happened next?" said Elizabeth.

"I talked to everyone who had ever known Annie . . . friends, neighbors . . . to try and get any clues as to where she might have gone. Since we'd both talked about moving to California, I had a pretty good suspicion that that was where she might have headed." Mrs. Robinson paused to smile at her daughter.

"I called everyone I could think of in California—the missing persons bureau, the police, the child welfare agencies—but no one had a Mary Robinson or Annie DeSalvo listed in their records."

"But my name is Mary Giaccio," said Mary.

"That's why I had so much trouble finding you," said her mother. "Annie changed her name to her mother's maiden name when she disappeared. She became Annie Giaccio and you were Mary Giaccio. Your real name is Mary Elizabeth Robinson."

Mary said her name out loud. "It's beautiful," she said, "and now I'll have it back."

"Tell us how you finally found Mary," said Amy.

Mrs. Robinson continued. "After I called all the local agencies and got nowhere, I decided my best bet was to move to California. That wasn't so easy, though. I had to work another six months in the restaurant to earn enough money." Mrs. Robinson sighed. "Those six months were probably the lowest point in my life. I'd been so accustomed to the noise and commotion of an active, happy four-year-old. Now I'd work a ten- or twelve-hour shift and come home to a silent, empty apartment. It was the worst sort of loneliness."

Mrs. Robinson turned to her daughter. "For a long time I left your room just as it was," she told her. "I couldn't even bear to pack up your things because that would mean I'd accepted your disappearance. Even after I'd been in California for several years, I still had all the boxes with your clothes and toys in them. By then I knew you'd long outgrown them. Anyway, when I finally had enough money saved, I moved to the West Coast and found a small apartment in Los Angeles. I took a job as a secretary. The money wasn't so good, but the office was very quiet so I had plenty of time to make phone calls."

Mrs. Robinson wiped her eyes and put her arm around her daughter. "As the time began to pass, so did my hope. Each year on your birthday, I would buy you a card and a gift, hoping that wherever you were, you knew that your mother still cared desperately for you. I even wrote to your father, hoping he could do something."

"You know where my father is?" said Mary.

"Of course," said Mrs. Robinson. "He lives in Baltimore with his second wife. You have two little stepbrothers, too."

Mary looked at her mother in amazement.

"Your father's going to be thrilled that we've finally found you. After I wrote to him about your disappearance, he and his wife were very concerned and very supportive."

"Wow," said Jessica, "this is a really exciting story. I feel like we're in a movie or something."

"What finally enabled you to find Mary?" said Mrs. Wakefield. "If Annie had changed her name, wasn't it virtually impossible?"

Mrs. Robinson nodded. "I had a strong suspicion that that was what happened," she said. "I wasn't even sure Annie still had Mary with her, but I knew that if I could somehow find Annie, I'd find Mary. Anyway last Wednesday Annie was arrested in Northern California for shoplifting. When they ran a background check on her, they discovered that her real last name was DeSalvo, and that she was wanted in Kansas on kidnapping charges. But Annie claimed that she'd never heard of Mary Robinson, and a search warrant revealed that she had no children living with her. Fortunately, a very quick-thinking police officer decided to see if a Mary Giaccio was listed with the state welfare agency." Mrs. Robinson squeezed her daughter's hand. "She was."

"I'll never forget the phone call from the police telling me that my daughter had been found. Oh, my poor little girl," she said, turning to Mary. "It must have been very difficult for you, wasn't it?"

Mary nodded sadly. "Annie told me that you died, but I never believed her. I just *knew* you were looking for me."

"Mary," said her mother, "do you still have the little gold and silver bracelet I gave you when you were a baby?"

Mary gasped. "You gave me that?" she said.

Her mother nodded. "It belonged to me as a girl."

Mary's eyes started to fill with tears. "But I gave it . . ."

"Of course she still has it," Elizabeth interrupted loudly. She poked Jessica in the ribs. "Right, Jess?"

Jessica sat up. It was obvious what Elizabeth expected of her. She carefully took the bracelet off her wrist and handed it to Mary. "Mary loaned this to me for a while," she explained.

Mary gratefully slid the bracelet back on.

"The welfare agency has told me that the Altmans would like to adopt Mary," said Mrs. Robinson.

Mary started to interrupt.

"But Elizabeth told me that she'd turned them down because she was still hoping that I'd find her," she continued.

Jessica stared at her sister and wondered where she'd gotten all this information.

"Do you live far from here?" asked Mrs. Wakefield.

"In a small town about two and a half hours from Sweet Valley," Mrs. Robinson replied. "My boss let me have the day off when I told him I'd found my daughter. Sweet Valley is a lovely place." She turned to her daughter. "I'm afraid Rushmore isn't quite as nice," she said.

"You're welcome to stay here tonight if you'd like," said Mrs. Wakefield.

Mrs. Robinson smiled. "That's very kind," she said.

Jessica was still staring at Elizabeth and marveling at the latest turn of events. "What about the Altmans?" she suddenly asked. "Do they know that Mary's real mother found her?"

"I was hoping to visit with them next," said Mrs. Robinson. "There's just so much catching up to do . . ." Her voice trailed off.

Mrs. Wakefield stood up briskly. "Girls," she said, "why don't we let Mary and her mother spend some time alone getting reacquainted? Perhaps they'd also like to go see the Altmans now."

"But it was just getting good," Jessica protested.

Mrs. Wakefield gave Jessica a meaningful look.

Jessica, Elizabeth, and Amy stood up reluctantly. "We'll see you later, Mary," said Elizabeth.

The door closed and Mary shyly faced her mother. She suddenly realized that the person she had fantasized about for so long was actually sitting next to her, and they didn't know the first thing about each other!

"We have a lot of talking to do, don't we?" said her mother.

Mary nodded.

"Do you think maybe we should go over and speak to the Altmans soon?" Mrs. Robinson added.

"I guess so," said Mary. It occurred to her that her mother was feeling as shy as she was.

There was an awkward pause. "Do you still like to eat chocolate ice cream?" Mrs. Robinson blurted.

Mary looked at her with surprise. "I *love* chocolate ice cream," she said. "How did you know?"

"Once when you were a little girl, I thought you were napping in your bed. Instead you had sneaked into the kitchen, pulled a chair over to the freezer, and taken out the chocolate ice cream. By the time I found you, the ice cream carton was empty and you were sound asleep on the kitchen floor!"

Mary laughed. "Really, Mom?" she said. At the word "mom," she stopped short. She repeated the word softly. "Mom."

The tears welled up in both their eyes. "That sounds good," said Mrs. Robinson. "I didn't think I'd ever hear that word again." She gave her daughter an affectionate squeeze and stood up. "Come on, Mary," she said. "Why don't you introduce me to the Altmans?"

Eleven

◇

Elizabeth, Amy, and Julie hung over Mr. Bowman's desk, studying the grade book he'd accidentally left open. Amy pointed to the middle of the page. "Bruce Patman's failed every test this marking period," she said.

"Too bad they don't give grades for good looks," Julie observed.

Elizabeth saw a tall shadow move across the room. "Amy, Julie," she hissed. The girls quickly stood up. They were relieved to see it was Mary. "Whew!" Elizabeth told her. "We thought you were Mr. Bowman."

Amy and Julie bent over the grade book again. It had been several days since Mary's mother had found her, and the excitement was finally starting to die down. There had been so much commotion at first. Everyone, including the Altmans, was thrilled and amazed. The local newspaper even did a story. Both Jessica and Elizabeth had been interviewed.

"What's up, Mary?" Elizabeth grinned.

"I was wondering if you were going home soon," Mary said. "I cleaned out my locker today, and I have about eighty pounds of stuff to carry to the Altmans."

"When's your last day?" asked Amy.

"Friday," said Mary. She looked down at the floor.

"Have you seen your new school yet?" Amy asked.

Mary shook her head. "No," she said.

Julie looked up from the grade book. "I don't believe this," she said. "Remember when Lila Fowler was bragging about how she'd gotten A's on her last three tests?" She pointed an accusing finger at the grade book. "She lied. She got two B's and a C+."

"Lila's father told her he'd buy her a horse if she did well. I wonder if he knows the truth," Mary said.

"He promised her a horse?" asked Elizabeth not believing what she had just heard.

"She's going at the end of the week to pick one out," Mary added.

"You think she'll let other people ride it?" Elizabeth asked. She couldn't imagine spending time with Lila. Still, if it meant a chance to ride her horse . . .

"Lila does what she wants." Julie sniffed. "She doesn't think about anyone else."

Elizabeth didn't say anything.

"Are you leaving soon?" Mary interrupted. She suddenly seemed to be in a hurry.

Elizabeth picked up her books. "Right now," she said distractedly. "Let's go."

As the girls headed across the parking lot, Elizabeth thought about what Mary had just told her. Lila was getting a horse! She wondered what it was going to look like and wished she could go with Lila when she picked it out. Besides, she knew so much about horses. Maybe Lila would appreciate her expert opinion.

"Elizabeth," Mary said, "remember when I first told you the story about my mother?"

Elizabeth noticed for the first time that Mary seemed upset about something.

"You said that if I wanted to talk to someone, to give you a call," Mary continued.

"What is it?" said Elizabeth. "Is something the matter?"

Mary slowed down. "It's just that . . ." Her eyes filled with tears. She began again. "I don't want to sound like I'm complaining or anything," she started to say.

"Mary," said Elizabeth firmly, "if something is bothering you, get it out. It doesn't do any good to hold it in."

"It's just that I'm going to miss Sweet Valley so much," she blurted. "Even though I'm happy to be with my mother, I feel like Sweet Valley is my home. All my friends are here."

"Have you told your mother this?" asked Elizabeth.

"I don't want her to think I'm ungrateful," Mary said. "After all the sacrifices she's made to find me . . ." She paused. "It's just that I've been shuffled around ever since I can remember. And Sweet Valley is the nicest place I've ever lived."

"Maybe your mother would be willing to move to Sweet Valley," Elizabeth suggested.

"I don't want to bother her about it," Mary said.

"But she told us all she liked it here, remember?" said Elizabeth.

Mary slowly nodded.

"It can't hurt to ask her," Elizabeth added.

Mary still looked as if she needed to be convinced. "I'd feel funny asking her," she said.

Elizabeth suddenly had a good idea. "Do you want me to talk to my mom about it?" she said.

Mary seemed relieved. "Would you?" she said.

"I'll ask my mother to call your mother tonight and see how she'd feel about moving to Sweet Valley," Elizabeth said. "She doesn't even have to mention that it was your idea."

"Elizabeth, thank you so much," Mary said gratefully.

Elizabeth smiled modestly. "I hope everything works out," she said. "I don't want you to leave, either."

That evening, after dinner, Elizabeth approached her mother and mentioned her conversation with Mary. Mrs. Wakefield was very understanding. "I'd be happy to call Mary's mother," she said. "We'd all love it if they decided to stay in Sweet Valley." She went into the bedroom and closed the door.

Mrs. Wakefield was on the phone for a long time. Elizabeth tried to listen through the door, but she could only hear snatches of the conversation.

Finally, Mrs. Wakefield opened the bedroom door. Elizabeth, who had been sitting in the hall the whole time, hopped up. "Well?" she said.

Mrs. Wakefield smiled. "She's going to speak to Mary about it," she said. "She had no idea how she felt."

Elizabeth gave her mother a hug. "Thanks, Mom," she said. "You're really the best."

"I try," said her mother cheerfully. She looked at her daughter and grinned. "Have you heard anything from the newspaper competition?" she asked.

"Nothing," said Elizabeth.

"You will," said Mrs. Wakefield. "I think you've got a winner there."

It was a crisp, sunny day one week later. The Unicorns, all clad in purple, were standing in the school cafeteria behind a card table piled high with cookbooks. On the other side of the table was a long line stretching out into the hall past the girls' bathroom.

"Do you believe this?" Jessica shouted above the noise. "I hope we have enough cookbooks." She handed one dollar in change to an eighth grade girl.

"Janet went to run off more," Ellen shouted

back. "If this keeps up, we'll be able to rent Dodger Stadium."

"Maybe we can use the money to hire a famous band," said Tamara. "I can see it now: The Unicorns present Diana Diamond.

The pile of cookbooks on the table continued to dwindle.

"Has anyone seen Mary?" asked Lila. "She's supposed to be here."

"She's out apartment-hunting with her mom," said Jessica.

"They decided to stay in Sweet Valley?" said Ellen.

Jessica nodded. "After my mom talked to Mary's mother, Mrs. Robinson called Mr. Altman. He offered to help Mrs. Robinson find a job and said she and Mary could stay with them until they were set up."

"The Altmans have been *so* sweet to Mary and her mother," said Tamara.

Jessica handed out the last cookbook. "One minute, please," she told the crowd. "We'll have more soon."

Janet came bustling through the cafeteria door. "Out of the way, everyone," she said. "Out of the way." She threw the stack of cookbooks onto the table.

Jessica looked up and saw Elizabeth walking toward the table. "Hi, Liz," she called. "Have you come to buy a cookbook?"

"Two." Her sister grinned. "One for Mom and one for Mr. Bowman."

"Mr. Bowman?" said Jessica.

"I owe him a thank you," Elizabeth said. She showed Jessica an official-looking letter.

"Elizabeth! *The Sweet Valley Sixers* won the contest!" Jessica exclaimed. "That's wonderful!"

"There's someone else I want to thank, too," Elizabeth said. She gave her sister a copy of the winning edition. "Do you notice anything new?" she asked.

Jessica slowly skimmed the paper. "Glamorous Gretchen Tyler Speaks to Students," she read. "By *Jessica* and Elizabeth Wakefield?"

"Read on," said Elizabeth.

Jessica examined the article. "I wrote this line about what she was wearing," she pointed. "And this next one too!"

"I got to thinking about what you said," Elizabeth told her. "You had a lot of good ideas."

Jessica couldn't have been more pleased. "Look, everyone," she said, waving the paper. "I'm a writer."

Mary ran up to the table. "Guess what, you all! We've found an apartment," she shouted. "I even have my own room, and it's close enough to walk to school."

"That's great, Mary!" said Elizabeth.

"Hey, how about some help back here?" called Janet. "We're being mobbed."

Mary and Jessica ducked behind the table. "How many cookbooks did you want again?" Jessica asked her sister.

"Two," Elizabeth repeated. "One for Mom and one for Mr. Bowman."

Mary reached for her purse. "Make that one," she said. "I'd like to buy the cookbook for your mom. May I?"

The twins looked at each other. "Sure, why not?" they chorused. Their mother would like that.

Just as the Unicorns had hoped, the cookbook sale was a huge success. Janet Howell was ecstatic. "I can't believe what a wonderful idea this was," she squealed. "We're going to have such a *fabulous* dance." Several of the Unicorns squealed back at her.

Jessica felt Lila tug on her sleeve. "Let's get out of here," she whispered. "Janet's about to make me gag."

The two girls slipped quietly out the cafeteria door. "Whew!" said Lila, leaning against the hall wall. "Sometimes Janet is too much. I mean, I love being a Unicorn and all that, but the Unicorns isn't my whole life. Besides, Dad promised he'd take me out later this afternoon to look at some more horses."

Jessica's eyes opened wide. "Are you really getting a horse?" she said.

"I've already looked at a few," Lila answered. "I can't decide which one I want, though."

"Where will you keep it?" asked Jessica.

"At a stable, silly," Lila answered.

"But who's going to feed it and clean the stall?" said Jessica.

Lila turned up her nose. "Not me." She shuddered. "All that stuff is included in the price."

"But don't you have to exercise it?" said Jessica. "A horse has to be exercised every day."

"It does?" said Lila.

Jessica nodded solemnly. "Exercised and brushed," she said. "The brushing takes at least thirty minutes. And then there's all the equipment that needs to be cleaned and polished." Jessica paused. "I guess we won't be seeing you too much anymore."

Lila stared at Jessica. "I think all those things are included," she said.

"I'd check if I were you," said Jessica with a knowing look.

"Since when do you know so much about horses?" said Lila.

"Elizabeth wanted to buy one," Jessica explained. "Mom said it was too expensive and then explained why they take up so much time."

There was an awkward pause in the conversation.

"Maybe you should call Elizabeth," said Jessica in her most helpful voice. "She knows everything about horses."

"I'll think about it." Lila sniffed. She turned abruptly and headed up the street toward her house.

"See you tomorrow," Jessica called.

Lila turned around with a funny look on her face. "Did you say when Elizabeth will be home?" she asked.

"Soon, probably," Jessica replied.

"Maybe I'll give her a call," said Lila. She tossed back her hair and continued up the street.

Jessica had a strange feeling in her stomach as she watched Lila disappear. Why did Lila want a horse if she didn't really care that much about them? Jessica shook her head and then turned toward home. She sure hoped Lila knew what she was getting into.

Will owning a horse be more than Lila Fowler can handle? Find out in Sweet Valley Twins #8, **FIRST PLACE.**